W9-AGJ-754

Back to the Cay

If... If... If I could get my sight back I'd try to put my feet on our cay and see it for the first time.

I had a picture in my mind of how it looked: a small "hombug" hump of white sand, palm trees sticking up from it, set in a horseshoe of coral, blue water lapping gently around it.

That's what Timothy saw from above, in heaven where he now lived: sun-spanked white water curling over the reef when the sea was running.

I'd felt it, tasted it, smelled it, heard it. I'd seen it through Timothy's eyes. Now I wanted to see it through my own.

Timothy

THEODORE TAYLOR

of the Cay

SCHOLASTIC INC.

New York   Toronto   London   Auckland   Sydney
Mexico City   New Delhi   Hong Kong   Buenos Aires

No part of this publication may be reproduced,
stored in a retrieval system, or transmitted in any form
or by any means, electronic, mechanical, photocopying,
recording, or otherwise, without written permission of
the publisher. For information regarding permission,
write to Harcourt, Inc., 6277 Sea Harbor Drive,
Orlando, FL 32887-6777.

ISBN-13: 978-0-545-08934-0
ISBN-10: 0-545-08934-4

Copyright © 1993 by Theodore Taylor.
Reader's guide copyright © 2007 by Harcourt, Inc.
All rights reserved. Published by Scholastic Inc.,
557 Broadway, New York, NY 10012,
by arrangement with Harcourt, Inc.
SCHOLASTIC and associated logos are trademarks
and/or registered trademarks of Scholastic Inc.

12 11 10 9 8 7 6 5 4 3 2   8 9 10 11 12 13/0

Printed in the U.S.A.   40

First Scholastic printing, April 2008

Designed by Trina Stahl
Text set in Stempel Garamond

For Caitlin Carroll—

wonderful, beautiful, scalawag granddaughter

APPRECIATION

My sincere thanks to ophthalmologist Dr. Roger Ohanesian of Laguna Beach, California, and to neurosurgeon Dr. Dennis Malkasian of Newport Beach, California, for their information on medical matters beyond my comprehension.

THEODORE TAYLOR
Laguna Beach, California
June 1993

CAY. A low sandy islet. But also extended to include large, higher islands with appreciable vegetation, e.g., Protestant Cay, Lovango Cay, Marina Cay, etc. CAY from Spanish lucayo; *Arawakan* cair: *island. Sometimes spelled and pronounced KEY.*

—*A DICTIONARY OF VIRGIN ISLANDS ENGLISH CREOLE*

1

USS *Sedgewick*

AUGUST 1942—The navy's Caribbean command received a priority dispatch from the USS *Sedgewick*:

RESCUED 12-YEAR-OLD BOY PHILLIP ENRIGHT AND HIS CAT FROM UNCHARTED CAY X SURVIVORS OF SS HATO TORPEDOED APRIL THIS YEAR X BOY AND CAT SEEM TO BE IN GOOD CONDITION X PROCEEDING CRISTOBAL X

The destroyer sped on toward Panama. She hummed and quivered along, pitching gently over the smooth sea, temporarily secured from hunting German U-boats.

Down in sick bay, the ship's hospital, I sat on a cold metal stool while the doctor checked me out. Took my temperature, looked in my mouth and ears, took my blood pressure.

I told him I felt fine.

With Stew under my arm, I'd been brought aboard from the rescue boat naked as a plucked pigeon, holding Timothy's wooden-handled knife as my only possession from our time on the island.

Lieutenant Robert Heath, the doctor, couldn't believe I'd survived, alone and blind, for almost two months on that remote patch of sand up in the Devil's Mouth.

"Timothy prepared me to live alone," I said. I owed my life to him.

"Who was Timothy?" Dr. Heath asked.

A cold disk was on my chest. He was listening to my heart. Stew Cat purred in my lap.

"An old black man from the island of Saint Thomas."

But he was much more than that. He was my guardian angel, then as well as now, protecting me from danger and mistakes. Though he was dead, he still talked to me in my darkness.

During that terrible moment, only yesterday, when the navy plane flew across the island and then went away, the sound dying like a bee buzz, Timothy looked down on me and said, "Don' warry, Phill-eep, dey'll be bock." I heard him distinctly.

"From Saint Thomas, eh?"

I looked in the direction of Dr. Heath's voice. He sounded young. "Yes. Timothy got me out of the water after our ship was sunk. A few minutes before, this tomcat had crawled aboard our raft. Just crawled up there like he owned it. Timothy didn't invite him."

I had to laugh about that, Timothy sometimes saying, "dis turrible cot."

"How long were you on the cay?"

"From sometime in April until today." Five months, I thought. I'd been told this was August 22, 1942, still a time of war. According to my own "time-can," into which I dropped a pebble or piece of shell each day, I'd been alone on the cay for forty-seven days.

"What happened to Timothy?"

"He died after a hurricane hit us. He used his whole body to protect me. Wind and flying debris tore him up. Killed him."

"What a shame," Dr. Heath said sympathetically.

Yes, it was.

"What did you eat all that time?" Dr. Heath asked, adding, "Lie back."

"Oh, fish and *langosta*, coconuts, sea-grape leaves . . ."

He made a *huhmp* sound, then laughed. "Not a bad diet at that."

Then he tapped around my stomach, telling me to cough. "You were blind before the ship was torpedoed?"

"No. I got hit on the head when we were abandoning it and lost my sight a few days later, on the raft."

He made that *huhmp* sound once more.

"Will I ever see again?" I asked.

"You'll have to talk to an eye doctor, but there's always a chance. You might need an operation." He paused, then said, "Phillip, I'm curious about something, really puzzled . . ."

"About what?"

"How did you manage for two months without that old man? How did you get food? You couldn't see."

"He'd made fishing poles for me. Strapped them to a palm tree before the hurricane hit. He'd planned for me to be alone. Planned everything. And I knew that whole island like I knew my house in Curaçao. After I buried him I put our hut back together and started a fire."

"Remarkable," said Dr. Heath. "Really remarkable . . ."

I had just been doing what Timothy had taught me.

"Now, sit up again. I'm going to tap your knees with a mallet to test your reflexes. Have you had that done before?"

"Yes."

I wondered how the doctor looked. How big was he, how old?

I'd been doing that all day, trying to imagine faces, starting with the two sailors who rescued me. I knew how Timothy looked, having seen him for two days before my sight failed. But now I had no way of telling age or looks except by voice.

The doctor tapped between my knee joints, then said, "Well, that's it. You're as healthy as anyone on this ship, a lot healthier than some. Remarkable."

"I was lucky," I admitted.

"Now, I've ordered a bland diet for you to begin with . . ."

I'd already had a milkshake.

". . . since your stomach probably won't be ready for hamburgers or steak . . ."

Oh yes, it is, I thought. Yes, it is! If I never have another fish it will be too soon.

". . . for a few days. So instead, things like rice and mashed potatoes and soup . . ."

"Can I have gravy?" Could I have every single thing that I'd missed on the cay? Everything. Macaroni and cheese. Hot dogs. Hamburgers. Ice cream. Candy.

He chuckled. "Yes, you can have gravy. Anything else?"

"Candy." That was something I'd really missed.

"Sure, what kind?"

"Hershey almond, Baby Ruth . . ."

"I'll have the ship's store guy come in."

"And will you feed my cat?"

"He's already been fed. Milk and rice. He was hungry. Anything else?"

I shook my head. "No, thank you."

"Glad to have you aboard," he said, and departed.

I think all the officers on that destroyer walked into sick bay that afternoon, and half the ship's crew, just to look at Stew Cat and me.

Lieutenant Commander Nathaniel Murry, USN, commanding officer of the *Sedgewick*, came in first. He said, "You're one lucky boy. Do you know how far we were off the beaten ship track?"

"No, sir."

"I got a report from Naval Intelligence that a Nazi U-boat was refueling from a Nicaraguan ship back up in here. Otherwise, I wouldn't have come near these lousy waters. They're beautiful but treacherous as a lit fuse. Coral reefs all over the place. They'll take your bottom out like it was cut with scissors."

"Where are we?" I asked.

"About a hundred seventy miles off the Nicaraguan and Honduran coasts, in waters called the Nicaraguan Rise. I came in as far as the Serranilla and Serrana banks . . ."

Timothy had mentioned those dangerous reefs.

". . . then headed east again. But turned back to get you. If that Catalina from Coco Solo hadn't spotted your smoke, I'd a been long gone . . ."

The Catalina was a twin-engine flying boat, I knew.

"Thanks for turning back."

"My pleasure."

He'd already sent a message to my parents in Curaçao, saying I'd been rescued. My father worked in the Dutch refinery on that island, off the coast of Venezuela. He was a petroleum engineer.

Carruthers and Gomez, the two sailors who'd brought the small rescue boat into the cay, had told him what they'd seen: my fire pile, the hut, my fishing poles.

"Where are we headed?" I asked.

"Cristobal, at the Panama Canal entrance. We'll hand you over to the naval hospital, get some fuel, fresh vegetables, milk, and eggs, and head out to sea again."

He went back to the bridge.

After the food tray was brought in, I spent the rest of the afternoon talking to the hospital corpsmen. They had dozens of questions. It was kind of fun being a celebrity.

———

On the cay, I usually knew when it was daylight because of the sun's warmth and when it was night because of the coolness. And, of course, your body tells you when to sleep. Aboard ship, I was too excited to go to sleep immediately after the announcement was made that the "smoking lamp" was out. Time to bed down, except for the duty watches. The corpsman assigned to me, who would also sleep in sick bay in case I needed anything, asked me if it was okay to turn out the light. I had to laugh.

Then he caught himself. "Oh, I forgot you can't see."

"That's okay." He wouldn't be the last to forget my blindness.

Quiet settled over the ship. Cool air blew down on me. The engines whined. The whole hull quivered at top speed. The corpsman said that when we were going twenty-five knots no torpedo could hit us.

I remember that night as being strange, one of many strange days and nights to come. I remember the feel of the bed and the clean sheets; the sounds and smells of the ship, knowing someone other than Timothy was just a few feet away. All of it strange. Most of all, I guess it was the knowledge that I wouldn't be alone anymore; that I wouldn't die on that forgotten, nameless cay, become a skeleton for someone to find someday.

There had been times when I almost gave up. At those times I "talked" to Timothy and he "answered" back. Who else was there to talk to, except Stew Cat? At first, I was lonely and frightened, but I'd always feel better after talking to Timothy. I'd imagine what he'd say to me and even imitate his voice. Imagination is a very powerful thing when you're alone and blind.

I finally went to sleep but awakened after a while, panicking on hearing the turbines' high-pitched whir. For a moment I didn't realize I was no longer on the soft sand floor of the hut, wrapped in deep silence.

Even Stew Cat was uneasy that night. He slept by my shoulder, snuggled against me.

I was awake for a long time, just thinking. Oddly

enough, one of the things I thought about, in addition to seeing my parents, was returning to the tiny island that I'd just left.

If . . . If . . . If I could get my sight back I'd try to put my feet on our cay and see it for the first time.

I had a picture in my mind of how it looked: a small "hombug" hump of white sand, palm trees sticking up from it, set in a horseshoe of coral, blue water lapping gently around it.

That's what Timothy saw from above, in heaven where he now lived: sun-spanked white water curling over the reef when the sea was running.

I'd felt it, tasted it, smelled it, heard it. I'd seen it through Timothy's eyes. Now I wanted to see it through my own.

2

Looking for Work

OCTOBER 1884—Tall schooner and bark masts, shorter raked sloop masts, and steamship smokestacks rose into the sodden island skies over St. Thomas Harbor as cries of "Buy mah feesh," and "Hey ba-nana, hey ba-nana," collided in the hot, humid air. Baskets of bunker coal, balancing on the heads of singing women, were going aboard steamers to feed fireboxes and boilers.

As Timothy moved through this noisy bustle, looking for work, other cargoes—in boxes and crates—were being loaded or unloaded. *Bluggoe*—a thick, fat plantain—and breadfruit and mangoes and pawpaw and bags of sweet yams came ashore from the down-island sloops, single-masters.

Clad only in pants made from a flour sack, his bare feet splashing over the smooth blocks of wharf stone, Timothy added his own voice. He shouted to bosses on the cluttered decks, offering his services this early morning. His earnest face and sinewy upper body, color of the bunker coal, glistened from raindrops.

"Sirrah, I wark hard, I do . . ."

Sometimes he made a few *øre*, a few Danish pennies, hand-carrying packages too fragile for wheelbarrows or pushcarts. But he was never satisfied with the handful of coins he took home to Hannah Gumbs, his foster mother.

He knew he was big enough, strong enough, even at age twelve, to lift some of the wooden crates that came out of the holds, or to push a loaded barrow into the long, low warehouses that faced the docks like huge piano keys. So far, none of the stevedore foremen, all as black as he was, had done more than scoff at him. The "bahsses" told him to come back when he grew up. Instead, his anger mounted each day.

The busy Danish port, located where the Atlantic Ocean and the Caribbean Sea met, lay in the track of vessels bound for South America from Europe, Africa, and the Atlantic states. The winds and tides led favorably to St. Thomas. Throw a bottle into the ocean off Senegal's Dakar and it would likely float to the Caribbean islands.

Steamers and ships under sail arrived daily. They moved slowly into the circular deep-water harbor, once a volcanic crater, now under the guns of two ancient forts.

Timothy stepped over the thick lines that secured the ships to land, careful not to get in the way of sweating men. They were guiding barrows down heavy planking.

He had passed four ships and now approached a big, trim white four-master that had just arrived. She flew the flag of Denmark and was called the *Amager*, out of Copenhagen.

She hadn't begun to work cargo as yet, but he stopped midships of her as two sailors bore a stretcher ashore. On it was a youth who appeared to be no older than himself. His left leg was laced between boards bound with twine.

Timothy thought he'd seen him before, a local boy, and he ran up to him, asking what had happened.

"De laig done broke," the victim said. His face was gray with pain. "I fell downg de laddah. Dey takin' me to de doctah."

He spoke in musical slave dialect, as did Timothy, though neither had ever been slaves.

Interested, Timothy walked alongside the stretcher bearers. "Yuh wark on dat ship?"

"Cobbin boy I be."

"Uh-huh," said Timothy, having a sudden idea. Cabin boy! That was where to start. "Yuh be goin' bock to 'er?"

"Dey paid me off. Cain't wark for six mont', mebbe, de mate said."

Timothy wished him good luck and wheeled around.

Heading back for the *Amager*, he thought about what a lowly cabin boy did—took care of the captain's and mate's rooms, did their laundry, served their meals, jumped at their most ridiculous wishes. But that was better than stirring Hannah Gumbs's wash kettle. What could he learn from stirring hot water over *bukra* clothes, white people's clothes?

Best of all, even if he was temporary, as a cabin boy he could sail the seas.

Timothy wanted, some outrageous day, to own his

own interisland schooner or sloop, be called "Coptin," and sail the Antilles chain to Barbados, or beyond, with freight and passengers. To get to be called "Coptin," the only school was the sea. That much he knew.

He'd visited the waterfront regularly since he was six or seven, perching on a bollard, the big iron mushroom over which mooring lines were looped, to watch whatever went on. When he had time off from helping Tante Hannah do her work for the rich folks who lived up in the hills, he usually came to the harbor. Already, he knew quite a lot about the ships and the men who sailed them.

They drew him past Kronprindsen's Gade, the beginning of Main Street; drew him past the old warehouses where pirates once stored their loot; drew him past the singing coal women. He'd sit on a bollard and daydream—listening, watching.

Truly wondrous things happened on that waterfront. Three times each year the "ice ship," a four-masted bark, would arrive from New England with its cargo of blocked ice cut from far northern lakes. Timothy loved to put his cheek against the sawdust-encased blocks, feel coldness he'd never known existed. The same ship carried barrels of rum north to a place called Boston. Once, a barrel being hoisted aboard dropped and busted. Then even the sea gulls got drunk.

He knew by now to get permission to board any ship. Once, he'd been kicked in his backside for boarding without asking.

The husky sailor standing at the rail of the *Amager*, bare to his belly button, wanted to know what Timothy's business was.

"Cobbin boy I be oskin' to be."

The sailor, an island man, grunted a "you'll be sorry" laugh, then said, "See de mate, 'e'll be bock soon."

Timothy promptly took up station between the two low deck houses and waited, dry mouthed and jittery, already tempted to leap down to the wharf and forget about his wild dreams. He forced himself to stand still.

Twenty minutes later, a chunky, squat *bukra*, blond haired and blue eyed, wearing a soiled white cap, returned to the *Amager* and looked at the boy standing between the mainmast and the mizzen; he listened briefly to the sailor, then walked over.

"What's your name?" He spoke English with a Danish accent and puffed a short cigar.

The official island language was English, in schools and otherwise. Light-skinned children were encouraged to go to school. Light-skinned girls needed to be educated, for domestic work in the mansions.

"Timothy, sirrah." Fright made his mouth flour dry.

"Last name!"

"I 'ave but one name, sirrah."

"How old?"

"Twelve, sirrah. I tink."

"You think?"

Hannah Gumbs had estimated his age. She didn't know for certain. Only his unknown mother knew.

"Yes, sirrah."

"You want to go to sea?"

"Yes, sirrah." Though he stood soldier stiff, his knees felt like sponges.

"Open your mouth." The mate came closer, blowing out strong smoke.

Timothy opened wide. He knew that slaves—like Tante Hannah, who'd been emancipated forty-one years before, in the Virgin Islands—had had to do that. Show their gums. Now he had to do it, too. He knew he did not have gum rot or other diseases. No sores.

"Bend your head, bend it."

The mate took one blunt fingernail to separate the hairs and examined Timothy's scalp. He was looking for lice.

"Spread your toes, nigra boy," the mate ordered.

Timothy bent down and opened his toes, feeling a humiliating surge of anger. But he dearly wanted the job. The mate was looking for chiggers now, he knew.

Taking a backward step to examine Timothy's whole body, the mate said, "You look strong enough to scrub a deck."

"Yes, sirrah."

"Have you ever been to school?"

"No, sirrah." With skin as black as a sea urchin, he wasn't exactly welcome.

"Can you read or write?"

"No, sirrah."

"Can you count?"

"Yes, sirrah." Timothy half lied. He could count to ten. Tante Hannah had taught him.

"All right, Timothy. Four *kroner* a month and keep. Do you have a shirt and shoes?"

Four Danish dollars a month, a fortune.

"I asked you if you had a shirt and shoes!" the mate thundered.

"I 'ave a shirt, sirrah."

"Get a pair of shoes. We're going to New York. Your feet'll freeze. I don't need frozen feet on this ship."

"Yes, sirrah."

The tobacco-smelling mate walked away and Timothy twirled around, permitting himself a wide smile, then leapt off the *Amager*. He began to run the second his feet hit stone; threaded and dodged through the light rain west toward "Back o' All," the poorest section of Charlotte Amalie, a squatter village.

Among the collection of one-room wooden shacks in Back o' All, where the coal carriers lived, was the one belonging to Hannah Gumbs. Feet flying in rhythm with his joy, Timothy hadn't known such excitement in however many years he'd been on earth.

Shoes? He'd never worn shoes in his life. The soles of his feet were tough as a leopard shark's back. But, yes, he'd find a way to get shoes. Nothing would stop him. Nothing would "harl" cold water on his soaring spirit at this moment.

He trotted along the inner edge of the harbor for a quarter mile, then turned sharply inland and began running up a low hill.

St. Thomas was a series of ridges and hills, some of them steep. Crown Mountain was fifteen hundred feet up. Some streets were no more than stone steps upward. Most of the rich people lived in the high hills, not the lowlands, wary of the hurricanes that visited occasionally. Everyone prayed that the island be spared at the beginning of the "tempis" season and prayed again in thanks at the end if it was bypassed.

Timothy ran on.

3

Panama

From the iron-railed bed in the Canal Zone's naval hospital I asked my mother, "Do you remember the old sailor we saw on deck the second day out, chipping paint?"

Timothy had been the oldest, biggest, and blackest of the SS *Hato* crew. Six-feet-two or -three when he stood up on our raft. His shoulders and arms were massive, heavily muscled from years of hard work. He hadn't shrunk very much from old age.

"No, I don't remember him."

I looked in my mother's direction. Without thinking, I'd been turning my head toward any sound for months. A bird, an aircraft, footsteps, a voice. Her voice. Sounds had become very important to me.

A hint of her favorite French perfume drifted over

from where she sat by the right edge of my bed. I remembered the delicate odor. Smells had also become
very important.

My mother was a slender lady with pale blue eyes
and pale skin. The last time I'd seen her, just a twisting
glimpse in a fiery red glow, we both had been spilling
out of the lifeboat into the dark water after the torpedo
hit the *Hato*.

"He was barefoot and wore a straw hat."

I wondered what she was wearing this day.

"That's his knife." I motioned to the bedside table
and reached over, groping for it.

"I don't think I saw him," she said.

Not far away a ship's horn bleated. A tugboat answered. Merchantmen and warships moved through the
canal night and day. Fighting was occurring throughout
the world, from Europe to the far Pacific. The once
peaceful Caribbean was a war zone.

"I think I saw him just before you sailed," my father said. "I wondered why a man that old was still
going to sea. He looked like he was sixty-five or
seventy . . ."

I turned toward his voice. Though he wasn't smoking
in that antiseptic room, a faint apple-flavored tobacco
aroma came from the foot of the bed. There was also a
touch of his bay-rum shaving lotion in the air. Reassuring
smells.

The last time I'd seen my father had been the previous
April. Tall and lonely, he stood on the seawall of Fort
Amsterdam, at Curaçao's harbor entrance. He was wav-
ing good-bye as the *Hato* put to sea. I had hated my
mother at that moment for taking me away from him.

But now he sounded as if no days had passed between us. Gentle of voice, always; slow and measured. He was a Virginian. My mother was from New Jersey.

"I think he was closer to seventy than sixty-five," I said, "but I'm not sure." There was a lifetime of things I didn't know about Timothy.

"Did he ever tell you why he was out there at that age?"

"The war. There was a shortage of experienced sailors, so he volunteered. You can't believe how much he knew about the Caribbean."

He knew the birds, the fish, the storms, the cays.

"You were lucky," my father said. "Very lucky."

That's what I'd been telling everyone.

We became silent for a moment. Had someone else been on the raft instead I might not have made it to that hospital bed.

My mother, whose dark hair always shone like glass, had sounded different from the moment she walked into the room. Subdued. Not a hint of the past's usual scolding in her voice. By tone she wasn't, for now, the taut, tense woman I'd always known.

They'd flown to Panama after the navy had told them, two days before, that I was alive and well. But blind. I'd fly back to Curaçao with them tomorrow. I really didn't need to be on that bed, but the nurses had ordered me to park there with Stew Cat and to stay out of the hallway.

My once long and tangled hair, turned straw blond (I was told) from the tropic sun, had been neatly cut. The nurses said I looked handsome and kidded me about going aboard the destroyer with no clothes on. They said I had a good tan all over and could get all the girls

I wanted, including them. They flirted with me even though I was years younger. I'd had a birthday on the cay, without cake or candles. But I felt older than twelve now, much older.

Stew Cat's leg drummed against the bedspread down by my feet. He was scratching an ear. The navy captain who ran the hospital had said he'd let Stew stay in the room, against all rules: "You two look like you belong together."

We did belong together. We'd shared a lot.

I kept looking toward my father. "His name was Timothy," I said. "That's the only name he had. Without him I wouldn't be here. He died and I buried him. He's now my guardian angel. We talk back and forth . . ."

They were silent, maybe thinking the sun had fried my brain. I'd buried another human in the sand and now talked to him. Maybe they didn't know what to say to me? Maybe they were still in shock that I was alive? Maybe . . .

The first few minutes after the nurse had shown them in, saying, "Here's that heartthrob son of yours" (which embarrassed me), my mother held me tightly. She said, over and over, "I'm so sorry, so sorry . . ." My face was wet with her tears.

Yet I felt uncomfortable in her arms. I didn't want her to be sorry for me. Timothy had never taken pity on me, and there were times when I'd thought I deserved it. But I learned from him that pity is often a deadly enemy.

It had been my mother's decision that we leave Curaçao to go back to our regular home in Virginia and what she thought was safety. But I'd long ago stopped blaming her for what happened.

As Timothy once said, "She started dis turrible wahr, eh, young bahss?" No, she hadn't started World War II, I knew. She was just frightened of it and wanted to flee once the U-boat attacks began.

"How did they find you?" my father wanted to know.

"Smoke from my fire pile was spotted by an aircraft working with the destroyer." It would take days to tell them everything that had happened on the raft and the cay.

First, I wanted to hear what happened to my mother after the torpedo hit, without warning, at three A.M., the darkest part of the night.

I remember that when I came up on deck with her the whole after part of the ship was on fire. Everything was red against the moonless night. There was a lot of fright and yelling. Then we were told to climb into the lifeboat so that it could be launched. As it was being lowered, the bow tilted sharply down, and we were thrown into the water.

My mother said, "I swam around trying to find you but you'd floated away. Then a sailor grabbed me and towed me back toward the lifeboat."

They'd gotten it into the water, after all.

"I fought him, Phillip. I didn't want to get into that boat without you. Then he slapped me and someone lifted me up—" Her voice broke again. "I thought you'd drowned and it was my fault, my fault . . ."

She said they had to hold her in the lifeboat to keep her from jumping overboard.

It was hard for me to imagine my mother jumping overboard and swimming off alone to find me. Yet I knew she was being truthful. She loved me, I also knew, though she seldom said so. People change in emergencies, Timothy taught me.

"We tacked back and forth all that day and the next one, going toward land. There wasn't much breeze. I thought of nothing but you and didn't care whether I lived or died . . ."

Then a tanker bound for Aruba, another of the Dutch islands, came along, and soon all the survivors of the *Hato*—except three—were safe.

"I told the tanker captain that you were in the water and had disappeared. I knew you had a life jacket and might still be alive. There were sharks . . ."

She stopped, voice fading.

"The captain then sent a message to the navy telling them the ship was sunk and that he'd picked up survivors," my father said evenly. He added, "I had no idea the *Hato* had gone down until that message was relayed."

He had a copy of it at home. He read it to me later:

PLS ADVISE PHILLIP ENRIGHT CARE CURA-
CAOSCHE PETROLEUM MAATSCHAPPIJ SS HATO
SUNK APPROXIMATELY 76 WEST 12 NORTH 6
APRIL X MRS. ENRIGHT SURVIVED IN GOOD
CONDITION X IS EN ROUTE ARUBA X SON
PHILLIP ENRIGHT BELIEVED MISSING X

He said he learned that the Dutch Navy had sent out a search plane from Curaçao and the American Navy sent three out of Coco Solo, here in Panama. Not even an oil slick was sighted. He had a pilot friend and they took off in a light plane and looked for me, too. They almost ran out of gas and had to land in Barranquilla, Colombia.

By that time, Timothy, Stew Cat, and I had drifted slowly northwest on our eight square feet of wood and barrels, toward the cays off Nicaragua.

"Tell us what happened on the raft, Phillip," my father said.

4

Back o' All

OCTOBER 1884—Hannah Gumbs was out behind the thatch-roofed shanty, using a long-handled wooden paddle to lift up steaming, dripping clothes. Charcoal from nearby Porto Rico glowed beneath the large cast-iron tub. Lye water boiled. Fumes rose from it and lodged in the light, warm rain, clearing nostrils in one whiff. Back o' All smelled of poverty, rain or shine.

Timothy shouted happily, "I be goin' to sea, Tante Hannah!. . ."

Hannah was not Timothy's aunt. She was no kin at all to him. She'd found him asleep on her doorstep at cockcrow time just before he was of crawling age. The note attached to the box, painfully written, said, "Timothy." Nothing else. But real aunt or not, she'd raised him like a son.

A faded blue bandanna on her head, she was wearing

a worn cotton blouse and a long skirt, no shoes. She turned and gazed at him. "Yuh goin' to 'prentice."

She'd been talking to a woodworker on Frenchman Bay Road, where she delivered wash, about Timothy becoming an apprentice. Learn to make furniture from Brazilian mahogany. A craftsman he would be. That was her hope.

"I be a cobbin boy, Tante Hannah," Timothy said stubbornly, hurt that she wasn't pleased he was going to make his way in the world. Grasp his own goal, at last.

A large, handsome woman with a face nearly as round as a pie, she narrowed her wise, deepset brown eyes. "Who said?" She was not one for *yaba-yaba* talk, senseless chatter.

After she was freed, she had refused to work for Estate Alborg, the sugar plantation where she was born and had lived most of her early life. She was proud and independent, though sometimes hungry. Her husband had died the year before she'd been blessed with Timothy. She never had a child of her own.

Until six years ago she had been a coal carrier, ninety-pound baskets of it pressing down on her padded head as she went up the steep gangways. Sweat had run down her body in thin rivers, even in winter. An *øre*, penny a basket, was what the singing coal girls got. They sang about hard life, keeping a rhythm with their steps.

Then her legs and neck gave out and she took up washing and ironing. Hannah Gumbs knew how cruel life could be. Timothy didn't, as yet—that was what her eyes were saying to him.

"De *bukra* mate o' dat schooner said. Four masts dat schooner, goin' to New Yawk. Dey be gibbin' me four *kroner* a mont' an' feed." His own eyes glittered with victory.

Hannah sighed, picked up an armful of dirty laundry, and dropped it into the pot. "Bes' yuh stay wit' me."

"I be goin', Tante Hannah," Timothy said again, picking up the paddle to stir the gray water for her.

"'Tis a hard life yuh oskin' foh," she said.

"No harder dan wark in de feels."

A slight nod said she might agree. And there wasn't that much field work on St. Thomas anymore. The early plantations were mostly in ruins.

"Yuh bes' wait to mek de chair an' table" was her final pronouncement.

Not wanting to look at her, knowing he'd miss her night and day, he looked at the huge pot. "De sea is whar I mus' go, Tante Hannah."

Her silence told him she would not interfere.

He added, "Someday I'll be a coptin. Den yuh can cease hard wark foh de *bukra* . . ."

Hannah laughed softly. "Don' tie de rope till you cotch de goat," she advised, pushing more charcoal under the pot.

Timothy knew what she meant: Don't get your hopes too high. He laughed back, "Coptin Timothy o' de schooner *Hannah Gumbs*, I be . . ."

She moved a few feet to take the boy into her arms. Neither paid any attention to the downpour or the fact that they were both getting soaked, head to foot. The sun would likely shine in a while and they'd dry off soon. It was nearing the end of the rainy hurricane season.

Then she stepped back, as the mate had done, to take another look at Timothy, but hers was a loving one.

She'd raised him well. Despite his lack of schooling, he was a smart boy. Wisdom seldom came out of books, anyway. He was strong and healthy, she knew.

A weedwoman, she'd used her knowledge of herbs and plants to keep him that way. Callaloo, the green leaves of the *dasheen* plant, always worked wonders at the supper table. Tea from *gritchee-gritchee* bush leaves kept his body tuned. A sliver of bitter sempervivum, the aloe plant, had fought off colds.

There were two dozen other bush wonders she knew about. The soapberry bush helped burns and scalds. So did fresh banana leaves. The toothache tree relieved jaw pain and "better-mahn-better" knocked down fever. Everyone in Back o' All came to Hannah Gumbs with physical complaints, leaving a few *øre* if they could afford it.

Yes, looking at him now, she knew she'd raised him strong and well; and now, sadly, it was time to let him go. She'd miss him as if he'd come from her own loins, but it was time. Time for him to be as proud and independent as she was.

He hurried off to tell everyone in Back o' All that he was going to be a cabin boy aboard the *Amager*. By nightfall, he'd located his two best adult friends, Charlie Bottle and Wobert Avril. They lived down island. He excitedly told them he was going to sea, at last.

5

The Raft

The *Hato*'s two sturdy rafts, one located on each stern quarter, were slotted wooden frameworks of boards about two inches thick, built over four empty but sealed oil drums. The slots let any water that splashed aboard fall back into the sea. Ours was the starboard raft, off the right side of the ship.

It was about four feet deep, I remember, and in the middle was a trapdoor so you could get to the galvanized tin box of supplies that was suspended between the drums. Also down there were two kegs, each holding five gallons of fresh water. Carefully doled out, the water could last four people a few weeks in high heat. Two people and a cat could share it for a month.

The box held emergency food such as hardtack, saltless biscuits almost as hard as rock; squares of chocolate wrapped in tinfoil; a signaling mirror and flares; a first-aid kit; fishing tackle; a kerosene lantern; and a box of sulfur matches in waterproof waxed paper.

I saw the trapdoor, the water kegs, and the tin box before I became blind.

The rafts were not made for comfort. They were made for survival.

I don't remember being hit on the head by the piece of timber that eventually caused my blindness. The first thing I knew I awakened on the raft with a stranger asking me, "Young bahss, how yuh feelin'?" For a moment I didn't recognize him as the old man I'd seen chipping paint the previous afternoon.

It was daylight by then, and a big black-and-gray cat sat nearby on the boards, licking his haunches.

The *Hato* was gone. So was my mother. I saw nothing but empty ocean everywhere I looked. The water was calm and blue. The sun glittered. The air was warm. The raft barely moved.

That first sight of the man I soon knew as Timothy was like waking from a nightmare and finding out it was true. In the moment before I realized he was from the *Hato* I thought maybe I was still in the ship's cabin, having a bad dream. No torpedo had hit us; no fire had roared. I hadn't even been in the lifeboat. But when he spoke, asking me how I felt, I knew it was no dream. There was no escape from him.

Just his face, let alone his size, frightened me. I immediately thought the deep, curved scar on his cheek was from a knife. My mother had said that West Indians were a violent people. His mouth was wide and his lips thick. Either scarred hand could have spanned a banjo—could have easily snapped me in two. But his voice was musical, West Indian–gentle, like a warm breeze in palm fronds; his smile was wide and toothy.

I remember weeping and throwing up.

On the third morning I awakened and thought it was still night. Puzzled, Timothy said, " 'Tis day."

I put my hand in front of my face and could not see it. I remember screaming.

I was blind.

6

Shoes

OCTOBER 1884—Donkeys brayed and cocks crowed when Timothy awakened at first light beside Tante Hannah on their shared plantain-leaf bedding. The only other sound, besides Tante Hannah's soft snoring, was the *zee-e-e-e-swees-te* of the banana quit. The ani, a long-tailed crow, wasn't awake yet, wasn't flying over the village with its shrill *weu-ik, weu-ik*. Wake up! Wake up!

Soon, human voices would float in from the outside as others in Back o' All awoke.

Tante Hannah rolled over.

A patchwork cloth hung between their sleeping space and the rest of the dirt-floored hut, which was always fragrant with the musky bundles of weeds. The cloth was raised during the day hours but at night formed the bedroom that Tante Hannah demanded.

She groaned and yawned and said, "G'marnin'."

Soon, there was a pungent smell of wood smoke and frying fish in Back o' All, helping to stifle the strong, ever-present odor of open sewage.

Water had to be lugged up the hill in buckets filled from a common well, then dumped into wooden barrels. After Timothy brushed his teeth with a soapvine chewstick, lugging water was his first chore of the day. Timothy had been carrying it since he was four or five. Wooden catchment troughs helped keep the barrels full during the rainy months, May to November.

Timothy never complained about down-and-out Back o' All, living in the hut, carrying water, or stirring the wash pot, squashing the *kakaroachee*. He knew no other life. Both Tante Hannah's parents had come from the Slave Coast of Africa. Compared to what they'd gone through—chained, starved, branded, robbed of every freedom—life was pleasant in Back o' All.

Aside from hurricanes and the sting of scorpions or centipedes or the *marley gumbeys*, the black wasps, and poison that might drip on him from the *machineel* trees if he stood beneath them in rain, there was no danger. No poisonous snakes existed. Even the bats that glided around the tamarind trees in the evening were friendly.

When ship arrivals were slack, Timothy roamed the beaches and mountains. From Crown Mountain he could see neighboring islands and cays. Even Porto Rico, to the west, was sometimes seen on clear days. Neighbors St. Croix and St. John loomed on the horizon. He longed to go beyond them.

Sometimes he played stickball or marbles with other Back o' All boys. One afternoon a week he went with Tante Hannah to gather herbs. Sometimes with Charlie

Bottle, who owned four cows and seven goats, to gather fodder on Thatch Cay and bring it back in a rowboat. One morning a week he'd go with Wobert Avril to net sprat or other fingerlings for bait, then bottom fish, with a hook and sinker.

But he was always drawn back to the waterfront. Time to time, he looked at the men off the down-island boats, wondering if one of them could be called *papa*. That was useless, of course, but Timothy firmly believed that the father he never knew, and would likely never know, had been a sailor. He'd be one, too.

He hadn't been below decks on a ship, let alone inside a master's cabin, and he couldn't believe the luxury in which the captain of the *Amager* lived. A round carpet was on the teak deck of the bedroom. He'd never seen such finery.

Dark woods and brass fixtures shone. The other boy had done a good job.

Nyborg, the stumpy, fair-haired mate, stood by the captain's double bed. "Let me see your hands, boy."

They were clean, scrubbed twice before he left Back o' All.

"Practice making the bed. He likes the corners exactly this way, you understand? Look down here, I say."

Timothy was looking at the whole bed, not just the corners.

A heavy hand slapped the back of his head.

"Yes, sirrah."

Then Nyborg led him into the room next door, a place for nautical charts and instruments. Timothy was wide-eyed.

"Scrub this deck every other day but touch nothing in here."

On the opposite side of the chart room was the captain's bathroom. Timothy had seen a sink and toilet before but never a bathtub. Wealth he'd never dreamed of.

"Scrub these spotless."

"Yes, sirrah," he breathed. He'd make them gleam.

Then Nyborg led him to the mate's quarters, where Nyborg himself lived, at the forward end of the after house. The instructions were the same for this smaller cabin, which lacked a tub and toilet.

After taking care of the captain and mate, Timothy was to help the cook. Do whatever he asked. Peel vegetables. Scrub pots.

Timothy believed he could do all these things. He would even enjoy them.

Nyborg ended the tour by showing him where he'd live—a narrow berth just off the galley in the forward house. His final words this first morning were, "I catch you stealing anything, I'll throw you overboard."

"Yes, sirrah." He'd yet to steal anything. Ever. Tante Hannah would have whopped him good.

His heartbeats slackened as the mate walked out of the galley. It wasn't so much what Nyborg said. It was the way he said it. It was the way the blue eyes went into Timothy's and out the back of his head. It was the way Nyborg held his hands. They looked as if they could form fists any second. Smash faces.

The cook was Porto Rican, Timothy guessed. He was standing by the stove. He waited until the mate was well out of range, then said, *"Muy malo."*

Timothy did not understand Spanish but the tone of the cook's voice, what his dark eyes were saying, and the gesture of his hands, were a clear warning: *Watch out*.

He nodded a thank-you and went aft to begin practice on making the master's bed, with the just-so corners.

On Wednesday, the day before the *Amager* was to sail, Tante Hannah took four *kroner* out of the hiding place in the shack and walked down the hill with Timothy.

"Ah'll pay yuh bock, Tante Hannah," he said, nodding his head as a promise.

"'Tis a gift," she said, smiling as they trudged along.

They finally turned in at Lilliendahl's, on Kronprindsen's Gade, and Hannah said, grandly, "Mah son needs shoes."

The clerk said, knowingly, "First pair ever?"

Hannah shrugged, deciding not to admit that outright.

The clerk measured Timothy's left foot and made a remark about the large size. Timothy *was* large for his age. Then he lifted a pair off the shelf and brought them over.

"Cowhide, made in *København*," the clerk said. They were brown, made in Copenhagen.

To Timothy they appeared to be made of gold, in heaven. Though he'd never told Tante Hannah he would like shoes, he'd thought about them. *Bukra* boys had shoes, though they didn't wear them all the time.

The right one slid on and the clerk said, "Stand up and walk around."

Timothy smiled at Tante Hannah and she nodded.

The shoe pinched but he thought that was what any shoe would do. He walked around, grinning at Tante Hannah. *His first shoe!*

"Let's try the left one," the clerk said, and Timothy sat down again.

In a moment he walked in a circle around Tante Hannah with both shoes on. His wide grin was enough reward for her this day.

She paid and they left Lilliendahl's.

Halfway up the hill, Timothy stopped, grin gone. "Mah feet hurt, Tante Hannah," he admitted. They were already blistered. Dismay was on his face.

She laughed and sat down by the path. "Gib 'em to me."

He sat down beside her as she worked them back and forth. "De feet say tek it easy. Dey don' know shoes."

In a few minutes they resumed the journey, Timothy barefoot again. But a short distance from Back o' All he put on the shoes so he could parade through the shantytown for everyone to see.

Timothy did not sleep well, thinking about boarding the *Amager* at dawn, knowing it would be months before he saw Tante Hannah and Back o' All again. Though he felt a hollowness about that, he smiled in the darkness about going to sea, at long last, on this day—the fore, main, and mizzen sails bellied out over his head. (He knew the names of the sails from watching and asking on the wharf.) Soon, he'd feel the rush of ocean beneath the *Amager*'s keel.

But he'd also fix the island and Tante Hannah in his mind and think of them often. He'd gone many places with her when she foraged for her weeds and he knew the island's beauty. There was color everywhere, the reds of the flame and frangipani trees, the yellows of the pudding pipe tree. Hibiscus were everywhere, in a half dozen colors. The perfume of flowers was constantly in the clean air. There was the warm water around the island, blue on the surface, clear beneath, washing white over the reefs. There were the powdery white sands of the beaches. He would hold them inside until he returned.

Before the first donkey bray and cockcrow, even before the first ribbons of canary yellow light from the east came over Grass Cay and Thatch Cay and Mariendahl, he poked Tante Hannah in the ribs and said, " 'Tis time to wake up."

She nodded and shook off her sleepiness, then went to the other side of the curtain to take off her nightdress and replace it with a blouse and skirt.

Outside, Timothy lifted the heavy kettle off the charcoal pile and pushed aside the night's feathery ashes, uncovering a few pieces that still glowed. It was the last time he'd ever perform this chore. After adding new charcoal he filled a pot with water and placed it over the coals. Tante Hannah would soon make bush tea. The tea and a few pieces of cassava bread spread with her orange marmalade would be their breakfast.

Last night Hannah had told Timothy he should wear his new store-bought pants and shirt going aboard the ship; he should dress nicely for the captain and mate, place his few personal belongings in a yam bag. So he went about doing that while the water boiled. He planned to wear his shoes and make sure the mate saw them.

Soon, saying little to each other, they started down the hill. With the low clouds' dimness he could not see the harbor. All of St. Thomas was shadowy, save a few early cooking fires.

As they reached the far-west end of the waterfront, even before the wharf began, Timothy stopped to put his shoes on. He'd daubed his blistered heels with Tante Hannah's salve and knew he could endure the pain until such time as he boarded the ship.

Tante Hannah finally spoke again. "Ah pray de good Lawd to keep yuh safe. Yuh do de same."

Timothy nodded but his attention was ahead, east along the wharf, toward the *Amager*. Though she was the fifth ship down, he should be able to see her tall masts in the gray light. But they didn't seem to be there.

He quickened his pace, ignoring the pain. Had she sailed? His ribs grew tight, his breath shortened. He began to run.

"Ah cain't see 'er!" he yelled frantically at Tante Hannah over his shoulder. There was panic in his yell. She struggled to keep up with him.

Finally, he reached the *Amager*'s berth. He couldn't believe it was empty. Panting, he looked south and saw the ship's white hull and masts standing out to sea between Hassel Island and Rupert Rock. Streaks of dawn illuminated her. The only steam tug in the harbor, the *Glory*, had her under tow, and Timothy knew her sails were being hoisted.

He was stunned. *They'd gone without him!* He should have come earlier. Tante Hannah puffed up beside him.

"Dere she is," he said, his voice high-pitched and helpless. "Dey left me . . ."

"Mebbe 'nudder boat cain cotch 'er," said Tante Hannah, breathing hard.

A voice behind them said, " 'Tis no use."

They turned.

The owner of the sloop tied up ahead of the *Amager*, a captain Timothy knew, said quietly, "Dey hired a *bukra* boy last night . . ."

The yam bag dropped by Timothy's feet, and his body became board stiff. His eyes were tightly closed, but not tightly enough to stop tears from leaking down.

He heard Tante Hannah say, "Anudder time dere will be." But her words did little to heal the ache inside Timothy. He felt empty, demolished.

A white boy had his job. Had he not made the captain's bed the right way? Was the brass not polished bright enough? Did the tub not shine?

Tante Hannah said, "Timothy, we be goin' home now."

He took another look at the *Amager* before her stern disappeared around the bulge of the island near Cowell's Point, and he nodded.

Then he bent to remove the shoes and tuck them under his arm. Tante Hannah told him to walk tall and straighten his shoulders.

7

Curaçao

Never having flown before, I wanted to watch the drifting, fluffy clouds, see the Caribbean below us. Perhaps a ship or a schooner would be cutting a white wake in the blue waters down there. Instead, I listened to the noisy twin engines, felt the vibrations of the fuselage, now and then a sickening bump.

Back in civilization, I was realizing more and more each day just how precious sight was. To look out any window was now useless. To look into a mirror was now useless. Even to look down at my hands or feet was useless. The darkness held me prisoner.

Over the engine's drone, my mother talked on and on about things that had happened the last six months. She'd done that, almost nonstop, since the moment she'd entered the hospital room in Panama. She felt guilty, my father said later.

"Oh, Phillip, I meant to tell you . . ."

Several hours later, I stepped down off the DC-3 ladder, holding Stew, Father guiding me.

Desert heat, so different from the cay, or the moist air of Panama, bounced off the runway. Whenever the brisk northeast wind stopped for a few hours, the heavy smell of oil from the refinery at Emmastad settled over the island and people held their noses. Willemstad didn't smell bad; it stank. This day I didn't mind the acrid odor. *You're home, safely home*, it said.

In the hospital, I'd had mixed feelings, several times, about even coming home without being able to see. How could I sail our small boat in the Schottegat, the inner harbor? Or fish off the beach at Avila? Go to the schooner wharf by myself? Just explore around the countryside, the way I'd done before the *Hato* and the cay?

I asked, "Has anything changed?" Dumb question. Things changed every hour.

"More ships every week. Four days ago a convoy came in with twenty-one tankers. The Allies want us to double aviation gas production," my father said.

Among the things I'd asked about on the destroyer were submarine attacks. The German U-boats were still out there. Not as many as in late winter and early spring, but ships were still being sunk.

My father's hand was loosely on my elbow as we walked to a taxi after clearing immigration and customs.

Timothy had done that for me, guided me, the first few weeks, until I learned how to use a stick and find my own way over the sands.

"The streets are crowded with sailors from every-

where. You'll hear five or six different languages," my
mother said.

I started to say I'd have liked to go over to busy
Breedestraat and see the sailors. Then I reminded myself,
See them? How could I? Sometimes even *I* forgot I was
blind.

I'd been to our main shopping area a thousand times.
My favorite shop was the Pinto and Vinck Ten Cent
Store, but I also liked the Yellow House and Liverpool
Drygoods of Arnold Valencia. In the doorway of the
Ten Cent Store was a poster of a pretty girl: *Ik Gerbruik
Pepsodent Tandpasta* (I Use Pepsodent Toothpaste),
with another message at her feet: *U Ook?* (You Too?).
Dutch words. I wondered if it was still there.

Someone would have to guide me over the Queen
Wilhelmina drawbridge, which spanned the Waaigat in-
let, then into the streets. Finding my way would take
time.

On the cay, I'd wondered which was worse: to be
born blind or to have your sight suddenly taken away.
I'd quickly decided that being born blind was the worst.
Never to see a bird, the sky, the sun or moon. Even for
a while.

The drive to Scharloo, the district in which we lived
near the ship channel that extended to the refinery, usually took about twenty minutes. Curaçao is only thirty-
eight miles long and nine wide at the widest, between
Jan Thiel Bay and Playa Canao. I well remembered how
that cross-island road looked the last time I'd seen it.
Here and there those strange *divi-divi* trees, their
branches shaped by the wind. All kinds of cactus, *machineel* trees, and manzanilla bushes along the road.

Most people think that every Caribbean island has lots of coconut palms, jungle plants, and wide, white-sand beaches. Our island was rocky, a desert type with cactus everywhere. Any palms we had were shipped in from South America. Our beaches were small, their sand coarse. There wasn't much rainfall, and tankers brought in fresh water as ballast.

"How be yuh healt'?" the cab driver asked, using English with a Creole twist. The moment he spoke I knew he was a native.

He'd heard about me: *Local Boy and Cat Found Alive*. The rescue operation had been in the papers as well as on radio. An Associated Press reporter had interviewed me in the hospital. *Time* magazine had called.

"I'm fine," I said.

I stroked a nervous Stew Cat as we scooted along. He'd have to adapt to a new land.

"Dat's good," the driver said.

The native islanders usually spoke Papiamentu among themselves. It was Spanish, Portuguese, Dutch, English, French, and more than a little African mixed into one language, the heritage of slavery. It was usually heard nowhere on earth except on Curaçao and her sister islands, Aruba and Bonaire.

I knew a few words. *Ayo* was "good-bye" and *mashi danke* was "thanks."

"Here we are," my mother said when the car stopped in the front of our house. My father made a joke about my luggage. I had no possessions except for Timothy's knife and the clothes on my back, bought the evening before in Panama City.

Our small stucco house, painted soft green with white trim and a red tile roof, was on the north edge of

Scharloo, well in back of the old mansions owned by the rich merchants. The oil company paid our rent.

Still holding Stew, I said, "Let me feel my way in," and moved across the uneven sidewalk. When I reached the iron gate and opened it, I fell down, Stew leaping out of my arms. I'd forgotten there was a step up.

"You okay?" my mother asked, and touched my shoulder.

On hands and knees, angry at myself, I said, "Yes." I'd fallen down hundreds of times on the cay. But the cement walk wasn't as forgiving as sand.

There were four steps up to the front door, I remembered, and I navigated them all right, finally entering the living room. To the left, against the left wall, rose the stairs to the second floor, where my room was. Almost dead ahead was the doorway to the dining room; beyond that, the small kitchen.

The smells and sounds of that gabled house came back—the sounds especially: floor creaks, the swish of the wooden-bladed ceiling fans, the wind chimes outside the back door. *Yes, I was home.*

I thought I knew where every piece of furniture was but right away tripped over the coffee table in front of the couch. There were two overstuffed chairs between a floor lamp by the opposite wall. I lost my bearings and went that way, falling over one chair, knocking the lamp down.

Suddenly, tears rolled over my cheeks. I hadn't cried since the day before I was rescued, hearing the sound of an airplane flying overhead, then dying away.

Knowing they were looking at me, I lashed out at my parents. "Stop watching me!" I yelled.

My father said quietly, "Okay, we won't."

I knew how I looked—hands outstretched, frustration on my face; angry at being blind.

"Would a cane help?" my mother asked.

I sighed and nodded.

"We'll get one for you this afternoon," my father said.

So, with everyone watching, I'd have to get around like an old man. Before, the only eyes focused on me had belonged to Timothy and Stew Cat.

"Just let me alone for a while," I said, sitting down in the chair I'd bumped into. "Where's Stew?"

One of them placed him in my lap.

"Would you like something to drink?" Mother asked.

I shook my head. I felt like a stranger in my own house.

They left the room and I could hear them talking in the kitchen, though they'd closed the door. They were talking about me, I was certain. What they needed to do was let me make my mistakes. Like Timothy had done.

Soon I smelled bacon frying. A little later my mother announced that lunch was ready, and I made my way into the dining room, felt around the table, and sat down in my own chair. I wasn't as helpless as they seemed to think.

On the cay, Timothy had placed my food—fish or *langosta* or coconut or boiled sea-grape leaves—on a driftwood plank. We both ate with our hands, naturally. The navy nurses had told me to feel for the plate, then use the fork. They made me guess what I was having. Sort of a game.

My parents had seen me eat the night before. I'd warned them I was messy.

"I made one of your favorites." A bacon, lettuce, and tomato sandwich. "And rice pudding, with raisins. Ice cream and chocolate-chip cookies for dessert."

I'm sure Timothy had watched me eat, seen me spilling food down my chest, but he'd never said a word.

Mother said, "Oops, some bacon came out."

"I'll find it," I said. I felt like yelling. It was in my lap.

Sitting down, Mother said, "Henrik called just before we left for Panama. He'd heard about you on the radio. He couldn't believe you'd been rescued."

That was Henrik all right. Always difficult to convince. I'd thought about Henrik van Boven now and then on the cay.

"He's really a true friend," my father said. "He took it hard when he learned you were missing."

"He wants to know when he can come over," Mother said.

I hesitated. I wasn't quite ready for Henrik. He'd want to know about every second, minute, and hour since last April.

"Let me set the clinic appointment first," my father said.

I nodded. They'd talked to the navy doctors about my problem.

The sandwich tasted great; I hadn't had a BLT since sitting at this same table months ago, in another life. A life I'd never have again.

Soon I groped my way upstairs, remembering when I'd taken them two at a time, up or down; then I turned into my bedroom, which was opposite the one belonging to my parents.

In my own room I was more certain of myself, knowing where everything was: the bed, the desk, the bureau, the closet, the bookshelves. I'd already been told that nothing had been touched since the morning we'd departed on the *Hato*.

I felt around. Everything was still in place, as they'd said.

I sat down on the edge of the bed, wondering what to do with myself. A moment later there was a thump, and then Stew Cat rubbed along my leg, purring. He was as lost as I was.

"Is there anything we can get you?"

My mother had followed me up. Maybe that's what she'd do from now on. Follow me everywhere.

I shook my head, looking toward the open door.

That whole first day and night at home I felt as if I didn't belong. On the cay I'd always had things to do, just to survive. Chores that had meaning. Here, I felt useless.

During the night I found myself missing the wind rustling in the thatched roof of the hut; missing the splash of the usually gentle surf; missing Timothy.

Here I was, secure in my own bed at last and not wanting to be there.

I asked Timothy, "What's wrong with me?"

There was no answer.

The next day Henrik van Boven visited. He'd also passed another birthday since I'd last seen him: he'd turned twelve, too. I sat on the front steps with Stew, waiting for him.

To me, he'd always looked very Dutch—straw-colored hair, moon face, and body on the chubby side. The van Bovens lived about seven blocks away. Henrik's father was city director of public works, and Henrik often sounded like his father, in charge of everything. Yet I liked him anyway; we'd had fun together.

Almost the moment I heard the gate squeak, he said, "You look different."

I knew I did. Still sun baked.

"And you're blind."

As if I didn't know it!

Laughing, I said, "Hi, Henrik."

"You're blind! That's what the newspaper said. Blind! Is that the cat?" Same old Henrik.

I said "Yes" to both questions.

By now he was no more than three feet away. Then I knew he'd sat down beside me. His voice came from the right. "Will you always be blind?"

"I hope not."

"All right, tell me everything."

"You said you read the newspapers."

"Yeah, but they always leave a lot of good stuff out."

I started with the torpedoing of the *Hato* and the raft, thinking I should just write it down on paper and hand it out to anyone who asked. People always had an idea being shipwrecked was like living on Robinson Crusoe's island.

When I told him about Timothy, he asked, "Why'd he call you 'young boss'?"

"Just habit, a leftover from slave days. He said he

called most white men 'bahss' instead of 'mister,' without even thinking . . ." I knew he didn't really feel they were his bosses. It was just his West Indian way of speaking. "After we became friends I asked him to call me Phillip."

I could hear his "Phill-eep" even now.

I talked with Henrik until he said he had to go home for dinner.

———

That night I again found it hard to sleep. My mind kept turning back to those first few hours when I'd recovered consciousness and found myself on the raft.

What I remembered most about that morning was Timothy's refusal to give me more than three small swallows of water. I'd hated him for it at the time.

A while later, I had a nightmare. A schooner that Timothy had once sailed on, the *Hettie Redd*, had been caught in a "tempis," a hurricane, off Antigua, and was breaking up. Timothy's feet were wedged in the rigging and he was drowning.

I woke up with my heart drumming. We'd talked about the *Hettie Redd* and a green-eyed girl named Jennifer Rankin.

I'd had dreams of Timothy while alone on the cay. Now I was having them at home.

8

Being a Slave

OCTOBER 1884—In the night quiet of Back o' All, from his floor mat Timothy asked Tante Hannah why the *bukra*s had left him. The *Amager* had been a stone in his belly all day. He had a broken heart, his disappointment so big he was drowning in it.

He hadn't known what to do with himself since early morning. For a while he'd walked in circles in Upper John and Dunko, staying away from Back o' All and the waterfront so no one would say, "Thot yuh gone to sea, boy."

About noon he'd returned home, silent and brooding, then had gone with Tante Hannah to deliver ironed wash to the estate on Frenchman Bay Road. They'd caught a ride part of the way on a friend's donkey cart, not returning until time for supper at twilight.

But he hadn't mentioned the *Amager* until this

49

moment, well after the evening meal, more than twelve hours after the ship had stood out to sea. Tante Hannah wisely hadn't brought it up either.

She sighed. "Can't say exactly why."

A gullie settled on the roof with a *cha-cha-chi* sound, its claws scratching the palm fronds.

Staring at the ceiling—annoyed that the gullie was up there, breaking into his thoughts—he asked if they'd left him because he was black. All day, he'd thought that must be the reason, the only reason.

"Mebbe." He heard another troubled sigh that went back to the Gulf of Guinea, the Slave Coast of Africa. "Sum o' dat but moh deeper. Way bock it goes."

She'd talked very little about her own past with him. Slave days. He'd guessed they were a painful subject with her, one she preferred to forget.

The fronds in the roof rattled. The gullie was walking around. Stupid bird.

Timothy guessed that slave ships had looked something like the *Amager*—beautiful above the main deck, but filled with horror and death below.

He waited patiently.

She was silent a long time, then for the next hour and more she talked about being a slave.

The slave ships had sailed for Africa out of America and England, out of France and Holland and Denmark; out of Portugal, out of Spain and Italy. Money was to be made in the New World, selling bodies.

The ships sailed with pots and pans and tools and guns, bolts of gaily colored cloth, cheap jewelry, and bottles of perfume. All of these were to trade to African chieftains for live black bodies. The ships first made land on the Grain Coast or the Gold Coast or the Ivory Coast—the Slave Coasts.

Timothy listened, thinking about trading pots and pans for human bodies.

The first hundred arrived in St. Thomas in 1673, almost two hundred years before Timothy was born. The king of Aquambon, located on the Gold Coast, had sold them to the Danes. For a while, St. Thomas was the chief slave port of the New World, Tante Hannah said.

The gullie scratched.

Tante Hannah's papa and mama, of the Ashanti tribe, had been walked out of Kade in clanking chains. They were naked. They had to walk a long way in high heat, but they were young and strong and they survived. She said others fell over and died, then were unchained and pushed off the paths for wild animals to eat.

Timothy listened, thinking of Tante Hannah's papa and mama naked and in chains, so frightened they found it hard to breathe. The gullie scratched again and Timothy was tempted to go outside and throw something at it.

Timothy had always heard it was horrible, that voyage across the Atlantic, but he hadn't known just how bad it was until this moment.

Tante Hannah said the "floating tombs" had bare wooden decks where the slaves were shackled, lying on their backs, many still naked. The cattle and hogs that were carried to slaughter for food weren't chained—only the slaves. But they sang songs of rebellion and love in tongues no white guard could understand.

The gullie cried *cha-cha-chi* and took off, flying upward.

In the soft darkness, Timothy again imagined those ships with their great white sails driving them westward, looking so pretty and peaceful, hiding the misery below.

Almost half the slaves died before they tied up in St. Thomas, Tante Hannah said. They were thrown overboard for the sharks to eat.

What happened then? Timothy wanted to know.

There was another long sigh. "De *bukras* fattened 'em up, doctahed 'em, den sol' em to wark de crops."

Her papa died nine years after being marched off the ship, at age thirty-one. Her mama lived five more years. "I warked longside 'er till she dropped ovah, weedin' cane. Papa died diggin' hols foh plantin'."

Chains still on them? he asked.

Tante Hannah laughed hollowly. "No, Timothy. No. Dere wuz nowhar to run."

They were never freed? he asked.

They died before that happened, she answered.

He'd been shown their conch-shelled graves at Estate Alborg. He'd been told that Master Alborg was a better master than most. But Tante Hannah still went back there only once a year, at Christmas, and then it was only because Timothy would be given a bag of candy from Denmark.

She sighed deeply and reached over to touch his hand.

"Ah 'member de day we got freedom. July third, 1848. De day before, we'd rung de estate bells an' blew on conch shells to tell de gobernor we wanted freedom. De nes' day, 'bout two tousand slaves circled 'roun Fort Frederik sayin' dey burn Saint Croix less dey freed. De gobernor came dere an' say, 'Yuh now free . . .' "

The wattle-and-daub huts where the slaves had lived

at Estate Alborg had long been destroyed. But slavery still hung over the plantation like an evil cloud.

Tante Hannah finally said, "Timothy, dey still tink we slaves, eben tho we free. Dey tink we don't 'mount to much. Dey still tink it an till dat change, we still in chains. Dat's why de *bukra* boy got your job."

So it *was* because he was black, not because he couldn't do the work. He thought about that awhile and then asked if he had any slave blood in him.

Tante Hannah's low laughter was turned inward as much as outward. "Ebry mahn, womahn, an' chile wit black skin in de New World 'as slave blood."

He asked her why they talked differently from the *bukra*s. "Dat, too, goes way bock," she said.

People from at least twenty-five tribes had landed in St. Thomas, many of them talking in different languages. To understand each other, they began to use bits and pieces of the white man's tongue. "Dey now call it pidgin Engleesh . . ."

Timothy stayed awake for another hour, thinking about what it would have been like to be a slave. He was too young for his own papa and mama, whoever they were, to have been slaves. But this night he felt Slave Coast blood in his veins.

No wonder there was something familiar about the chants of the coal women at the wharves.

No wonder he felt his own feet move when Tante Hannah danced on Emancipation Day, celebrating the anniversary of the day when the governor freed the slaves.

Now he knew it was all inside him and would never go away.

9

The Clinic

My father called the refinery clinic. The doctors there, all from Holland, were the best on the island. They served sixteen thousand workers.

"At two o'clock," I heard him repeat.

When he placed the phone down, I asked, "Do they have an eye doctor?"

"Yes."

The name of the eye doctor was Boomstra, and he seemed more interested in what had happened on the cay than in my eyes. Kept asking me how I'd survived.

After X rays were taken and developed, he hummed to himself while examining me, asking me exactly when I thought my sight had begun to fade, asking my mother if she'd seen the blow to my head. She hadn't.

It was Timothy who'd figured out what had glanced off the back of my skull: a piece of timber that had come loose when the lifeboat was launched. It had hung up awhile, then fell on me when I was in the water.

"How much swelling was there?" Boomstra asked, speaking with a thick Dutch accent. He sounded elderly. I pictured him with white hair, a white mustache, a big nose, and thick glasses.

I said there was a big lump for a few days, and I'd had bad headaches.

He finally asked all of us if he could speak frankly. He knew how old I was. I wasn't a child. Even before my parents answered I said, "Yes."

He nodded and chose his words carefully. "If you want to see again I think you face a very serious operation by a neurosurgeon. And there is no guarantee that it will be successful."

My mother gasped. "No guarantee?"

"The optic nerve is in the back of the head. I believe it was damaged by whatever struck the skull."

My heart beat faster. I'd had my tonsils out when I was eight. "You said serious . . ."

"Phillip, any operation where the body is invaded has risks."

Always to the point, my father asked, "Where would you recommend we take Phillip?"

"Columbia Presbyterian Hospital, in New York. There's a specialist on staff who is world famous for this type of procedure."

"Tell us about the operation," my father said.

"I'd rather let an expert explain it."

My mother's voice wavered as she asked, "Has he done this before—to a child?"

I didn't feel like a child anymore.

Dr. Boomstra replied, "I don't know. But he is world famous. Lars Pohl."

After a silence, my father said, "We need to think and talk about it."

Boomstra said, "I understand."

We thanked him and a few minutes later were on our way back to Scharloo.

As we drove along, all of us thinking of the same thing—the surgeon's knife—my father said, "If Dr. Boomstra was right, the final decision will be yours, Phillip. We'll both tell you what we think but it'll be your decision."

"We'll get other opinions," my mother interrupted.

"Of course," he answered.

"Where?" I asked.

"Anywhere," my mother said. "And other doctors may not agree with Boomstra. They may have other ideas. It may be just a simple operation."

Or I might never see again, I thought.

We talked back and forth for days, and then, in October, made the decision to go to New York. My father called Boomstra, asking him to contact the "world-famous" neurosurgeon Dr. Pohl.

"When will we go?" I asked.

"As soon as possible. We'll fly," he said, making it sound like an order.

I'd noticed he seemed more forceful since the *Hato* sinking. He didn't let my mother push him around. This time she didn't object to flying. She had no desire to end up in the sea again.

A while later, after Boomstra called back, my father phoned Pan American Airways and booked a flight for my mother and me the next week. Only two seats were available; he'd follow two days later. Stew would have to be boarded in a kennel.

10

New York City

New York City had always sounded exciting. I'd seen it in photographs and picture-show newsreels. On the radio I'd listened as the announcer said: "From our studios in New York, we bring you . . ." Now I could only feel it, hear it, smell it, on this cool October morning.

Rush hour, footsteps, people around us everywhere. Traffic starting, stopping. Horns blowing. Squeaks and rumbles below us as we walked over subway gratings. Exhaust fumes mixed with food odors. Constant noise, so different from the quiet of the cay.

Living in sleepy Virginia, I'd always wanted to take a train to New York. See Rockefeller Center, Radio City Music Hall. See Times Square at night. Walk along Fifth Avenue and Broadway.

Now I was here. Our hotel was the Commodore, on Forty-second Street, by Grand Central, in the middle of Manhattan.

That first morning, Mother decided to take a walk before we caught the subway to Dr. Pohl's office at Columbia Presbyterian. I think she wanted to take my mind off what might be said. I held her arm tightly, bumped now and then by pedestrians.

She'd been to New York before and described things as we went up crowded Forty-second. When we crossed Fifth Avenue, she said, "Look, there's one of those big double-decker buses . . ."

Like others, she kept forgetting I couldn't see.

Ever since that afternoon in the refinery clinic I'd thought a lot about what the neurosurgeon *might* say: "I'm sorry, Phillip, an operation won't help." Then I'd go to a school for the blind. Learn braille. Be sightless forever.

So I wasn't very much interested in double-decker buses. Going to Dr. Pohl's, holding a large envelope with the Curaçao X rays, I was frightened of the unknown.

Soon we went down the steep stairs into the subway tunnel, me taking uncertain steps, bumped again by people. The thick air smelled like battery acid. The trains screeched. The platform shook. I wanted to go back to the street.

I'll forever remember that long ride, sitting there swaying side to side, listening to the harsh noises. Uneasy as the train jerked and burrowed underground, I hoped we could ride a bus back.

Aboveground thirty minutes later, we were told that Dr. Pohl was in surgery but wanted more X rays before talking to us anyway. The ones taken in Curaçao were probably okay, his nurse said, but he wanted his own. He'd talk to us after looking at them and after my father arrived. That would be tomorrow. The nurse escorted us downstairs so my skull could be photographed.

Another twenty minutes with the technician saying to move my head this way or that way and we were back out on 168th Street, soon to board a bus for midtown.

Crazy as it sounded, there was something I wanted to do this humid day. Every since I'd seen it in a magazine I'd wanted to go up in the Empire State Building, the tallest in the world. A hundred and two stories, I remembered, over a thousand feet up. The magazine said that on a clear day you could see in a circle for two hundred miles.

When I said I wanted to go up there, my mother said, "But, Phillip, you can't see anything."

That I well knew, but we could take the elevator up just the same, and she could tell me what was out there—New Jersey, Brooklyn, Connecticut; the rivers, the ocean. "I want to feel the wind."

"Feel the wind? That doesn't make sense, Phillip," she said.

I was silent a moment, then said, "Haven't you ever done anything that didn't make sense?"

"I try not to," she said.

On the eighth floor of the Commodore, the night sounds from below were muffled. We'd had dinner two hours earlier and the nine o'clock news had just finished, the announcer saying that the marines were fighting a desperate battle against Japanese troops on Guadalcanal

Island, in the Pacific. The war was always present these days.

My mother switched off the radio, and I heard the click of her bedside lamp. Then she said good-night.

I said good-night too, thought awhile, then added, "I want to go back to the cay."

I'm sure she was frowning over at me. "Back to that island? I should think you'd never want to see it again."

"I didn't see it, Mother. I couldn't see it. That's why I want to go back—if the operation works."

"You can't be serious."

"I am. I want to walk around it, see where our hut was. See where I fished and dove for *langosta*. See Timothy's grave . . ."

She was silent a moment, then said, "His grave? It would seem healthier to me if you put it all out of your mind. Think only about getting your sight back. That's the main thing, not some tiny, remote island and a grave."

I doubted she'd ever understand. I said, "Mother, I want to thank him again."

She said, "You can't thank a dead person. You have to say thanks while they're alive . . ."

I kept silent.

"Phillip, he's dead—gone! There are no such things as guardian angels. There is no communication from heaven. Or from hell. Maybe you need another kind of doctor." There was anger in her voice.

I didn't answer.

Then she let out a long sigh and said, "When I unpacked your bag last night I found that knife in the bottom of it. Any reason you brought it along?"

"For luck," I said.

"A knife will bring you luck?"

"Timothy's knife." I thought it might.

"I think you're possessed by that man. You know how many times you've talked about him this past week?"

"I loved him," I said. "I love him now."

"You loved a Negro?"

"Yes."

It was as good a time as any, up in that hotel room, far from the Caribbean, to ask, finally, "Why don't you like black people?"

There was a moment of silence. She seemed about to explode. Then: "Did I ever say that?"

"You've said it in many ways, Mother. You'd make a face when I mentioned them. You told me to stay away from them . . ."

"They're different, don't you know that? My grandmother knew it, my mother knew it, and I know it. They have their own way of life. That's why they live in a separate part of town."

Her grandmother knew it, her mother knew it, and she knew it?

"Maybe it's because we don't want them to live in our section," I said.

"That's nonsense. Most don't have the money to live in our area. And they wouldn't live around us even if they could."

"Why not?" I asked.

"They have their own music, their own food, their own way of dressing, their own way of talking, and they live happily in their own sections. Do you think Timothy would want to live in Scharloo?"

I had no idea. "He might." But I didn't think he'd want to live next door to my mother.

"Are you afraid of them?" I asked.

"Let's just say I'm uncomfortable around them."

"Why? Did any black person ever do anything to you?"

"Phillip, don't question me," she flared, the old tightness back in her voice.

"Timothy said that under the skin we're all the same."

"I'm not interested in what Timothy had to say about this subject."

That ended the conversation.

11

Obeah

OCTOBER 1884—In early morning, still thinking about what Tante Hannah had said the night before about slavery, Timothy was fishing in Wobert Avril's rowboat. They were anchored near the coral reefs off Galosh Point, hand-lining for grouper at about thirty-five feet. Also down there were snapper, jack, mackerel, barracuda, and bonito. But fat grouper was what they were after.

Later, when the sun was fully out, they'd be able to see the fan-covered reefs and the fish.

Though he was sometimes foggy headed after a night with Demon Rum, old Wobert knew more about fish and birds and the sea than any man alive. Timothy was sure of it. He knew the winds and the stars and the reefs. He knew the islands and cays all the way south to Trin-

64

idad and Tobago, west to the Morants and Providencia. Timothy wanted his knowledge.

Tante Hannah had told Timothy, "Lissen to de ol' mahn, all de ol' mahn, iffen dey wise. Den yuh be wise."

Timothy thought of Wobert as his grandfather. He looked like a grandfather and talked like a grandfather. He often said, "Riddle me dis, or riddle me dat . . ."

Wobert told the best stories about fish and *jumbi*s, the evil spirits. Timothy both believed them and didn't believe them at the same time. Once, Wobert told him about catching a "barra" that was seven feet long. Timothy didn't think that any barracuda could be seven feet long. Four feet, maybe even five. Never seven.

Wobert showed him the palm of his right hand where the line had cut an inch deep until the barra broke it. And one morning about ten o'clock, Wobert said, breathlessly, "Look downg, look downg!" Timothy looked down and there was a seven-foot barracuda swimming slowly by them, one big eye cocked at the boat.

Wobert's best story about *jumbi*s was the one where Mama Geeches battled a *jumbi* under the stairwell of Hotel 1829. She was the "obeah" lady who lived in Back o' All and cast spells. The smoke *jumbi* was threatening to burn the hotel down until Mama Geeches, who was less than four feet tall, fought it and killed it with ground-up butterflies. Her throat and private parts had gotten scratched. Wobert had seen her throat scratches but not the others.

Until he'd gotten a knee busted in a storm off Barbuda, Wobert had sailed the Caribbean and offshore Atlantic for forty-four years. "Fo'ty-foe," he reminded everybody. Now his right knee was about as stiff and useless as a gravestone. He walked peg legged, like his right one was wooden. He could no longer get around a sailing-ship deck.

Timothy liked to sail into the harbor when they had a good catch, Wobert blowing his conch shell, *A-ooouuuu, a-ooouuuu*, to announce they had fish for sale.

Timothy wanted to talk about being a slave, but Wobert had just accidentally hooked a goatfish in the gill and was taking great care in getting it off the hook, using a cloth to protect his hands from the sharp fins.

"Nevah eat dis feesh. Don' eben let 'im stick yuh."

Timothy had heard Wobert say that every time he'd hooked an unwanted goatfish. Wobert had an old man's habit of repeating himself. As he was expected to do, Timothy asked, "Why not?"

"Pozen. 'E meks whot yuh call 'gut-rot.' Dere's a Sponish word for it, *ciga*-somethin', dat means de same. Mek yuh veree sick."

Then Timothy knew that Wobert, who had a wizened face like a dark brown nutmeg, and crinkled gray hair, would tell him, once again, that goatfish could be poison off St. Thomas but good to eat off Guadalupe. Wobert had an idea that goatfish nibbled sour coral on some reefs, not on others.

Timothy listened him out, then said the *Amager* had sailed without him.

Wobert, looking sharply from under his straw hat's brim, said, "I heerd so. Mebbe yuh better off stayin' here. Doin' land wark. Lookit whot the sea did to me." He slapped the busted leg. Though he was sixty-odd, his eyes were those of a young eagle, sharp as knife tips.

Timothy shook his head to disagree, then said he'd keep trying and changed the subject. "Yuh eber a slave, Wobert?"

Clouds were drifting in and the sun had come up, dropping yellow patches over the waters east of Galosh Point. A vagrant easterly breeze notched the blue surface, rippling it, causing tiny waves to slap against the boat's port side with a hollow sound.

Wobert's sound was a half chuckle. He said, "Oh, yass; oh, yass . . ." Strange, like Tante Hannah, he'd never talked about it before, as if it was something to be ashamed of. He had been twenty the year of Emancipation, he said; it was the same year he'd gone to sea.

Timothy jerked on his line and soon landed a three-pound grouper that drummed the boat's bottom with its tail. Unhooked, it still flapped as Timothy angled the stringer cord through the gills and out of the mouth, then tossed it back overboard.

"Why yuh ast?"

Timothy said Tante Hannah had said how it was with her.

Wobert said, "We all de same. Me an' her jus' got lucky we didn't 'ave to mek the trip across. We born in Saint Thomas."

Timothy said he wanted to know how it was with Wobert when he was a boy. Wobert laughed again. "Dey made me tend chickens when ah was five. Ah had *caca* 'tween my toes till I was twelve."

Caca was chicken dung, Timothy knew.

"Den day put me in de feels, holing. We dug holes 'bout four feet square, an' nine inches deep, wid heavy hoes. By noon, mah arms ached. But Ah'd git a kick in mah behin' if Ah slowed up. Next we forked manure into de holes, den planted cane cuttins . . ."

"Yuh do dat ebry day?"

"Only at plantin' time. Res' o' de time de chillun weeded till de cane was cut. Den de fires begun in de boilin' house, to make molasses . . ."

"Yuh warked all de time?" Timothy asked.

"Sunup to sundown 'cept on Sunday. In boilin' time, de mahn warked ebry day."

Wobert talked about how it was to be a slave almost until noon, when they sailed back toward shore. The last thing he said about it was, "Yuh lucky, bein' born after Freedom Day."

That was true, Timothy realized.

Wobert added, "One ting I larned when I was a chicken boy—black hens lay white eggs," then he cackled and cackled, slapping his useless leg. "Riddle me dat."

Timothy wasn't sure what he meant. He'd ask Tante Hannah later.

He trudged to Back o' All with two fat groupers. One to give away, one to cook.

———

A layer of floating whitish wood smoke made a roof over Back o' All just before sunset and trapped the rich food smells that came from the open fires outside the huts.

Tante Hannah was almost ready to take the boiling *maufé* sauce—diced pork, tomatoes, and onions, and cooked flaked grouper—from the embers and pour it over *fungi*, cornmeal shaped into balls. She stirred in some of her own handpicked bay leaves and ginger, then took a sniff. Nodding, she went back into the hut and brought out two plates.

The fair dawn weather had continued into the twilight, the trade wind picking up a cool edge in late afternoon. The heat of the charcoal would feel good once they sat down to eat.

Soon, Tante Hannah served the simple meal, saying a blessing over it before they took their first bites.

While they were eating, Mama Geeches came over uninvited and sat down by Tante Hannah. The birdlike, tiny woman, always dressed in lavender and wearing silver rings on her baby-sized fingers, was paid to chase *jumbi*s. She was also paid to bring good luck.

It was said that Loupgarau, the man-spirit who took off his clothes and flew by night in a ball of fire, sucking blood from his victims, played with Mama Geeches just after she was born. He introduced her to the world of spirits, including Soucayant, the female Loupgarau.

Mama Geeches lived two huts down. She stared moodily into the fire. She shook her head when Tante Hannah offered her some *maufé* and *fungi*.

Timothy had always been afraid of her, tiny though she was. He was afraid of her old-country spells and magic. There were many stories about Mama Geeches. She was neither young nor old, neither living nor dead. Even *bukra*s came down from their mansions in the hills to visit Mama Geeches for one reason or another.

Finally, looking over at Timothy with sleepy dark eyes that were barely visible in the crimson glow, she said, "Pay me two *kroner* an' Ah'll sink de *Amager*." Her voice was that of a little girl.

Was there anyone on the whole island who didn't

know he'd been left behind? Mama Geeches seemed to hear everything that went on. The *Amager* was likely two hundred miles along her northerly course to New York. *Sink her?*

Tante Hannah bristled at the thought. "We'll do no such ting."

Mama Geeches, still looking intently at Timothy, said, "Pay me two *kroner* an' Ah'll git yuh a good ship."

Frowning, Tante Hannah said, carefully and uneasily, "'E'll git 'is own ship when 'tis time."

Mama Geeches slowly rotated her head toward Tante Hannah to threaten, "An' it'll be a goat-mout' ship." A bad-luck ship.

Retreating, Tante Hannah said she couldn't afford two *kroner*, having just spent her savings on shoes and pants.

Mama Geeches rose and moved off into the shadows, soundless as a mongoose, for which Timothy was grateful. He let out a long *whew*, relieved.

Another such breath came from Tante Hannah.

As Mama Geeches moved beyond what they thought was hearing range, Tante Hannah said, bravely, "Don' fret, yuh know she just a silly obeah womahn." But the tense look on her face said something else. It said that she was as afraid of the miniature *jumbi*-chaser as he was. Always had been, always would be.

Like *bamboola* drums, Mama Geeches got into everybody's head and gullet with her words. Because they were mysterious words, powerful words, everybody listened.

Within his memory, Tante Hannah had paid Mama Geeches to rid their yard and hut of visiting *jumbi*s several times. Once, Mama Geeches sat on the doorstep holding a chicken in her lap, talking to the chicken until it fell asleep. She sat there all night and at daybreak the chicken awakened and the *jumbi*, circling the hut like a rope of fog, departed.

Another time a *jumbi* got into Tante Hannah's left foot through a spider-bite hole and wouldn't leave. The foot swelled up like a big red banana. Weeds wouldn't cure it but Mama Geeches did. She went to the graveyard and got some dust, then added ground-up chalk and pieces of snakeroot. Tante Hannah soaked her foot all night in the nearly boiling cure water, and by morning the *jumbi* swelling had gone.

So Timothy, too, believed in Mama Geeches's obeah, and that night on the plantain leaves he decided to start saving *øre* until he had two *kroner*, to make sure he wouldn't get a goat-mout' ship when he finally went to sea.

12

Dr. Pohl

Dr. Lars Pohl's hand was firm when it shook mine, and his voice was deep and strong, even gruff. His shaving lotion smelled crisp. He soon asked the same questions that Dr. Boomstra had asked, taking notes, I think, but he wasn't as much interested in what happened on the island. He was more concerned about the headaches I'd had.

Later, my parents described him as square faced and gray haired, a large man with bushy eyebrows and a big nose. His cheeks were red. He was Danish. They said he had powerful hands with long fingers. Along with his diplomas, my father said, there were autographed pictures on his office walls. Babe Ruth and Lou Gehrig, baseball stars of that time, among them.

He shone a light into my eyes, asking what I could see. Nothing. He felt the back of my head.

"Will I always be blind?" Instantly, I didn't want him to answer that question.

He paused, likely studying my face, then said, "To tell you the truth, Phillip, I can't say. There's a possibility that what has happened can't be reversed. In fact, there are a variety of possibilities here . . ." He paused again.

A variety of possibilities? Doctor talk. I said, "But—"

"Let me finish! I've studied your X rays but cannot judge from them just how much damage has been done . . ."

My father had arrived in the morning, and now I felt his hand on my shoulder. He squeezed it to remind me that he was there.

"How can you tell?" I asked.

"Another procedure, and I'll get to that. But first let me try to explain, as simply as possible, what I *think*, just *think*, happened to you, Phillip. I believe that whatever struck you in the back of the head caused internal bleeding in the area of the occipital lobes . . ."

I frowned. *What were those?*

"The function of the occipital lobes is to receive sensory information from the optic nerves, the eye nerves, and process it. They are the center of the brain for vision. Your eyes are only cameras. I think you have an AV malformation, an artery-vein malformation . . ."

My frown must have deepened.

"I'm showing pictures in a medical book to your parents and will also explain them to you. . . . Here are the normal blood vessels in Plate Eighty-four, like little bending hoses. Now we see them damaged in Plate Eighty-five. They look like clusters of grapes. With stalks. A vessel bleeds and stops and clots. Pressure builds up and another starts to bleed, and it clots. Another does the same thing—seeps and clots. I think these clots, these grape clusters, are causing your problem."

He paused to let it all sink in.

"What can you do to fix them?" I asked.

"Every one of the damaged multiple little vessels would have to be cauterized and then repaired with a metal clip or stitch to stop the bleeding. Each one would have to be identified. A very delicate operation, working up against the brain."

"And that would fix it?" I asked.

"Perhaps. But it's a very long, risky operation, requiring a team of surgeons."

I liked the way he was talking directly to me.

". . . I've done nine so far, all on adults, all within days or weeks of the injury. You've had yours for going on six months . . ."

My father asked, "What kind of success have you had?"

Dr. Pohl did not hesitate. "Three out of nine regained partial vision. One died on the operating table. One is brain damaged. So five are still as blind as the day I performed surgery on them . . ."

"Three out of nine," my mother said, a quiver in her voice.

Dr. Pohl replied, "Phillip's age may possibly be to his advantage." Then he said to me, "But I doubt if you'll ever have a complete return of vision."

"The three that were successful—how much vision did they have?" I asked.

"Two had eighty, one ninety percent with glasses. Not that much at night."

Ninety percent with glasses. I'd be able to see most things, read, move around without a cane.

I guess he was studying my face when he said, very clearly, "I repeat that there is risk, Phillip. I have to be honest with you and your parents. Major risk. This will be inside your skull, against the brain . . ."

Inside my skull? Against my brain?

"My biggest concern is with the lining of the brain. I'll be a fraction of an inch away from three very important vascular structures, blood channels. I'll skip the scientific names for them, but they carry much of the blood away from the brain and return it to the heart. Any of the three could have been injured at the time of the accident or could be injured during surgery. Your life could be lost; you could be paralyzed . . ."

My mother said, "I don't think we need to hear any more, Dr. Pohl."

It was my vision he was talking about, not hers. I asked, "What happened with the one person who died?"

"Hemorrhage that we couldn't stop."

A ruptured blood vessel.

"What you have here, Phillip, and Mr. and Mrs. Enright, is a choice between remaining blind as a relatively functional person for an undetermined period versus the possibility of an acute problem during immediate surgery that may leave you, and I repeat, paralyzed and vegetative, or dead . . ."

My mother said firmly, "With those options, Phillip will have to remain blind."

My father said, "Not so quick, Grace. He has to have a voice in the decision. What do you mean by 'undetermined period,' Doctor? That sounds scary . . ."

"Well, until we can take a look at the problem, beyond X rays, there's no way of knowing exactly how severe it is. It just takes a small amount of blood to disturb the function of the brain. There can be lasting side effects."

Silence from all three of us. We knew he meant that I might die anyway, from malformation.

He said, "You don't need to decide today, but each day that goes by lessens the chance for any success."

"Eight didn't die," I said.

"But five can't see," my mother said.

There was another long pause, then my father said, "Doctor, Phillip faced life-and-death decisions on that island. He survived . . ."

I knew he was talking to my mother as well. Saying to her, *Stop thinking of him as a child.*

". . . so he has the right to make the decision. It's his sight, his life . . ."

I sat there, knowing they were looking at me, waiting for me to say something. I'd thought a lot about this moment since the session in Dr. Boomstra's office, thought about it on the plane to New York, thought about it almost all the time I was awake since arriving. I wanted to know exactly what was going to happen and said so.

The doctor hesitated. Later, he told me he'd hesitated because he was afraid I'd become frightened. "How much do you want to know?"

I said, "I'd like to know how you get there."

Dr. Pohl hesitated again, then I heard a deep sigh. "All right. Simply because you did survive alone on that island, and that means to me you're mentally strong, I'll tell you. I'll also tell you, Phillip, that most adults wouldn't want to hear about the exact procedures."

I was physically strong but didn't know about the mental part.

"Stop me whenever you wish," he said.

I nodded.

"You'll be put to sleep and your respiration and blood pressure will be carefully watched. You'll be placed on your belly because we have to have complete access to the back of your head . . ."

As if he'd written it down, word for word, I remember what he told me: The first step would be an incision on the back of my skull . . . a straight incision; then instruments would pull the skin of my scalp to the side, to expose the skullbone.

After that, he'd make four or more holes in my skull.

"How do you make them?" I asked.

"With a hand drill."

I heard my mother moan.

"Like woodworkers use?"

"Exactly."

He then used a lot of scientific words like *transverse venous sinus* and *superior saggital sinus*, without even thinking we didn't know them, then brought himself up short, apologizing.

"What we'll do, Phillip, if you make the decision to go ahead, is place a guide between the four burr holes, and then pull a gigli saw, a wire saw, back and forth until the necessary bone cuts are made to provide an oblong window for surgery . . ."

A window in my skull?

"The second procedure will be to go in through that window and try to repair the blood vessels. . . ."

"Will you put that window part back?"

He laughed a little, softly. "Yes, we certainly will. When we replace it, we'll make up a paste out of shavings from the bone, to hold the piece in place. Then your own cells will grow together, though you'll always feel a little depression back there."

"How long will I be in the hospital?"

"You should be on your feet in two days, but we'll keep you for about a month for observation. If everything goes well, your vision will return in about two weeks."

"What about aftereffects?" my father asked.

"Probably some residual headaches, but they should go away after a while. A possibility of some seizures, but they can be controlled with drugs if they occur."

"Seizures?" my father said. "Similar to epilepsy?"

"Exactly. As you likely know, there are two types. Petit mal and grand mal. The petits are more of a nuisance than anything else. You might be drinking soup and for a split second will stop the spoon in midair. The grand mals are a lot more serious; the patient loses consciousness."

We had a boy at school with epilepsy. Without warning he'd pass out, fall down, then his muscles would jerk. He might froth at the mouth.

"Drugs can control them and eventually they'll go away. But you have to take the drugs regularly," Dr. Pohl said.

"What causes them?" I asked.

"Disturbances of the brain's electrical activity. In your case there will have been quite a shock to your circuits."

I'd heard enough.

"It's a very serious, risky operation, eight to twelve

hours long, and you may lose your life, Phillip. Or as I said before, become almost totally incapacitated."

"Or I may see again," I said.

"Yes," he agreed.

"You said ninety percent for one of the adults."

"No guarantee of that percentage," he said, bluntly. "Another thing, there could be problems even if the operation is successful—infection of the wound, a blood clot forming on the surface or inside the brain . . ."

"You don't sound too optimistic," my father said.

"I'm being honest with all of you," the doctor said.

Finally, after a few minutes, I said, "Can I think about it?" Never had I been so scared. Not on the raft or on the cay.

"Of course, but the sooner you make the decision the better. If you decide to go ahead, we'll need to do an pneumo-encephalogram. That's the procedure I mentioned before."

Again I was lost in the medical terms. "What's that?"

"More X rays. We'll put you in a chair and inject air into your spine, then rotate the chair in different directions. By putting air in, we can see more of what the problem is, then go in and operate . . ."

13

The Decision

We left his office at Columbia Presbyterian and talked about what Dr. Pohl had said the rest of the day and into the night.

I'm not sure when I went to sleep or when my parents did, but I remember thinking that what I wanted to do in life required vision. Even more than that: I never wanted to question myself when I was older about not accepting the challenge of risky surgery.

Scared that I'd lose my life on the operating table, I also thought of those seven adults who'd survived without brain damage. Four were still blind, but they'd tried to do something about it. Should I?

I awakened early that morning and lay there trying to go over everything Dr. Pohl had said. The traffic noises from Forty-second Street were faint.

I finally asked Timothy, "What should I do?"

"No rain, no rainbow," he replied.

I remember him also saying, "Night bring day." Sorrow during darkness, joy in the morning.

Finally, I asked my parents, "Are you awake?"

They were.

I took a deep breath. "I'm going ahead with the operation," I said.

"Are you certain?" my father asked.

"Yes, I want to go back to the cay."

"Oh, Phillip, you said that the other night. You have to have more than that for a reason," my mother said. "*You have to! . . .*" I could tell she was almost in tears.

"He has to have a goal, Grace," Father said, quietly but firmly. The decision was made.

He called Dr. Pohl just after nine o'clock and the pneumo-encephalogram X rays were taken that afternoon.

14

Bark *Gertrude Theismann*

APRIL 1886—In sultry late spring, Timothy was rowing Charlie Bottle's boat, laden with the grass they'd cut on Thatch Cay—which wasn't really a cay at all; fresh water was beneath its soil. The grass was for Charlie's livestock.

A sheen of sweat coated Timothy's supple body, making it look oiled. As he pulled the oars, his arm and belly muscles flowed like warm molasses. He'd filled out since the *Amager*, had added two inches in height.

He said, "Almost two year I 'ave tried. Dey say, 'Grow up, boy . . .' "

"Tell de mates an' coptins you be sixteen. Den yuh may git de job." Charlie Bottle's bloodshot eyes were locked on Hannah Gumbs's foster son.

Timothy frowned. Tante Hannah had always said, "Talk d'truth an' shame de debbil."

"Long's yuh tell 'em yuh fo'teen, dey say, 'Grow up, boy,' an' yuh got no wark."

Timothy nodded. Charlie Bottle was known for his wisdom, like Tante Hannah and Wobert Avril.

"An' yuh look sixteen, yuh do. Yuh a big boy now," said Charlie Bottle.

There was no breeze to fill sail this day. The knock of the oarlocks, the slap of water against the bow, were the only sounds as they went south toward Coki Bay, where Charlie's donkey cart awaited.

Timothy nodded again. That was true, he thought. Big as most men. Strong as most men.

Six days later, he announced to Tante Hannah that he was finally going to sea, on a bark bound for Rio de Janeiro. He'd heard of that place down in Brazil. He'd seen ships from there. He'd heard their Portuguese-speaking sailors.

Tante Hannah congratulated him with a sad face.

Even though he'd signed an official-looking paper with his *X* (all the words on the document meaningless to him), Timothy still wasn't sure that he was finally going to sea in the four-masted *Gertrude Theismann*, a ship that called Philadelphia home port. She was square-rigged, except for fore-and-aft sails on her aftermast, some jibs and headsails forward. She was the color of milk; pretty as a giant butterfly.

He remembered Mama Geeches saying two years ago he'd get a goat-mout' ship, a bad-luck ship, unless he or Tante Hannah paid her two *kroner*. They'd talked about it and decided that was an idle threat. How could Mama

Geeches know one ship from another, which was a bad-luck or a good-luck ship? Mama Geeches had gone too far that time. But he thought about her as he signed his *X*.

Because of what had happened with the *Amager*, Timothy didn't actually believe he was going out in the *Gertrude Theismann* until Luther Oisten, the boatswain, boss of the deck, issued him a blanket and the cook handed over a tin plate, fork, and knife.

His board-slatted bunk, soiled straw-filled mattress, and stained pillow were in the cramped pineboard fo'c'sle, in the forward end of the ship, which was also quarters for five other sailors. A table and two benches were against the after bulkhead. The room smelled of sweat but compared to Back o' All it was rich-man living.

Aft of the fo'c'sle was the galley, with a sliding panel, the "pie hole," for food to be passed through. The food was good beyond belief. Timothy had helped load it.

But the first words that the bo'sun said to Timothy were harsh: "Yuh jump when I tell yuh, nigra boy. Yuh green as soursop, an' watch yuh step on deck less yuh die out dere . . ." He was a slim, thin-nosed Bajan from Barbados Island, in the Windwards above Trinidad and Tobago. With a few cups of *bukra* blood in him, his skin was more brown than black. He wore a sheathed knife at his right hip.

"Yes, sirrah," Timothy replied, standing stiffly, already frightened of Luther Oisten.

"Now, turn to," Luther ordered. "Go to work, loadin' stores."

Timothy had always heard that second mates and bo'suns, often one and the same on sailing ships, were naturally mean. Too well he remembered Nyborg, of the *Amager*. Maybe they had to be mean to survive. The white chief mate, Tanner, had seemed pleasant enough, as had the captain. They left the bully talk to the Bajan.

When the Bajan moved off, Horace Simpson, the oldest of the four Negro sailors, suggested, "Do as he tell yuh." White-haired Horace Simpson, from Alabama, reminded Timothy of Charlie Bottle. He was short and stocky.

Timothy said, "Yes, sirrah," though ordinary sailors were never sirs.

The only white man in the fo'c'sle was Phelps. Bewhiskered, face like an ax, he dipped snuff. He'd hurt his foot and wasn't able to go aloft. Horace said of him, "Worthless."

Thomas Sanders was the cook-steward. He not only cooked but took care of the captain's and mate's cabins. The final crewman was ship's carpenter Deets, another white man, in charge of the steam-deck engine, which hauled up the sails, ran the pumps, and occasionally heaved in the anchors. He slept in the carpentry shop.

Those were the *bukra*s and the blacks aboard the *Theismann*. Eleven of them, including the master.

She'd loaded coal in Virginia, twenty-five hundred tons of it, and had off-loaded six hundred in St. Thomas. She'd also off-loaded general cargo boxes. In Rio, she'd pick up bagged coffee after cleaning her holds of anthracite dust. Deliver to a Philadelphia warehouse.

Now it was time to sail south.

Timothy had been unable to sleep during the night and heard the cook stirring next door even before cockcrow. A smell of wood smoke soon crept into the fo'c'sle, then a stronger whiff of burning coal; and finally, Luther, a dim figure in the open doorway, shouted, "Turn to!" and the snoring in the fo'c'sle stopped abruptly.

Timothy washed his face in a bucket of lukewarm water on deck and helped ready the ship for sea until breakfast was called. A pot of oatmeal was passed through the pie hole, followed by a slice of ham and one egg each, boiled potatoes, bread, and a pot of coffee. Timothy had never eaten so well.

As dawn came up, feathery golden clouds to the east, there was a head of steam in the donkey engine boiler; the halyards were laid out and coiled, ready to pull sails up; the *Glory* came alongside, and the captain gave orders to depart.

––––––––––

Timothy saw Tante Hannah standing on the wharf in the thin new light and waved to her, proud that she'd seen him at work singling up the mooring lines. He fought back tears, knowing it might be months before he'd see her again.

The towing hawser was passed to the *Glory* and the bark separated from land.

Within minutes, halyards were bent around the gypsyheads on either end of the winch, powered by the donkey engine, the Bajan yelling, "Heave away!" The upper tops'ls were soon set; then the lower tops'ls were sheeted home. After that the headsails went up.

Timothy was too busy taking orders to do more than glance back at the figure of Tante Hannah. She was still on the wharf.

Abeam of Water Island, the *Glory* said good-bye and

soon the topgallants and royals and all the fore-and-aft canvases were bellying out in the light easterly breeze.

The *Gertrude Theismann* was underway for Rio.

Her master, Captain Donald Roberts, of Maine, wrote in his journal, which was kept separate from the terse official log:

JUNE 8, 1886, 7:30 A.M.—Departed St. Thomas without incident. I'm always quite ready to leave port though Mr. Tanner reported only one fight here amongst the crew. The usual reason, Demon Rum.

While in port I added a West Indian apprentice seaman to replace the boy who fell out of the mizzen crosstrees, 160 feet above deck. (He landed like a bag of beans, and I buried him sewed in canvas off Florida, as noted in the log.)

This new apprentice is named Timothy. He said he would work from St. Thomas to Rio and back for the price of a pair of shoes, a bargain I could not pass up. Though polite, he is a bold black boy. When I called him "Tim," he said, "Sirrah Coptin, I 'ave but one name, 'tis Timothy." I almost bashed his mouth but then laughed inwardly. After watching him on deck the past three days I believe he may turn out to be a good seaman. He knows what happened to the last boy and will likely be careful aloft.

For obvious reasons I did not tell him we won't be returning to Philadelphia via St. Thomas. I will take on additional stores and make the run from Rio to the Delaware capes in one long voyage, God willing. Unless my schedule is changed, this vessel will proceed to

*Le Havre, France, after we reload in Philadelphia. The
boy will have to make his own way back to the Caribbean unless he wants to cross the Atlantic with me,
and I with him. I've ordered Luther to train him well.*

Four o'clock in the afternoon: all gear had been
stowed away long ago, the decks hosed to wash down
shore dust, and countless other ship-keeping chores
performed.

Not until that time—work done for the day and
night, unless there was a shift of sails—could Timothy
fully take it all in, the sights and sounds. Then he realized
he was indeed at sea; that the life he'd always wanted
had finally begun. He would not awaken in Back o' All
tomorrow.

The sea had turned deep blue as the hours passed,
and the white thunderheads had reached higher in the
western sky. There was a rhythmic creaking and wearing
as the *Theismann* gently rose and fell, a hiss of water
under her bow.

He went forward and straddled the bowsprit for a
long while, looking ahead, almost hypnotized. Then he
turned and looked up at the bellied sails—the skysails,
the royals, the topgallants.

He walked along the tar-seamed warm deck aft to
stand at the starboard rail near the big steering wheel,
watching Horace Simpson move the spokes, wondering
how long it would be before the captain and mate trusted
him at the helm. Mr. Tanner had the watch.

The captain was still in the whites he'd worn on
departure—white shirt, white pants, white shoes—and
a blue cap, from which peeked curls of white hair. He
was smoking a pipe and had a faraway look on his face.

Timothy knew, for many reasons, that he'd never look so fancy as this captain. When he got his own schooner, whenever that would be, he'd have bare feet and his pants might be tattered, his shirt worn and stained. But how he dressed would not matter. What would matter was being master of the *Hannah Gumbs*.

For three days he'd thought about the *bukra* boy he'd replaced, the one who'd fallen off the mizzen cross-trees. They were so high up the mast his breath squeezed just thinking about them. The crosstrees were a pair of horizontal timbers that supported the tiny highest platform on the mizzenmast. From the deck they looked like they might scrape the clouds.

Sooner or later Timothy knew he'd have to climb all the masts to furl sail against the yards, going up in fair weather or raging storms. Hang on when the ship plunged or rolled. He wondered, this first day out, when the seas were calm and the breeze light, if he had the courage to make the climb. *Do it now!*

For about twenty minutes he stared up at the succession of rope ladders that led to the yard of the mizzen royal, then took a deep breath and swung up on the first hard rope rung of the shrouds, eyes glued to the top of the mast. It was moving slowly back and forth, a dizzying two hundred feet above. Heart pounding, he saw the spread of sails, then the sky over the slender "pole," the highest section of the mast. He continued to climb.

Horace Simpson saw him high above the deck and shouted, "Don't look down!"

Captain Roberts turned his head slightly to watch.

Pausing a moment, mounting fear binding his chest, Timothy thought of backing down, one foot at a time. But he knew that Horace and probably the chief mate and the captain were looking up at him. Maybe others by now. Then suddenly, thinking about where he was, clinging to the ratlines, he looked down and *froze*.

Unable to go up, unable to go down, he was like a fly caught in glue. Though the late afternoon was warm, cold sweat popped out on his forehead.

There was dead silence from below. He guessed they all knew what had happened. They'd sailed a long time and had seen it happen before.

Would someone come up and get him down? Would they tie a rope around him and lower away? He'd be disgraced his first day at sea. Luther would say, "Nigra boy, yuh lie; yuh a chil', yuh not sixteen . . . ," then laugh at him.

Tante Hannah had been right, "Don' nevah lie . . ."

He knew that his fear would not let his body move, no matter what he said to it. His hands, grasping the rope rungs, were already aching. His legs felt like stones. Surely he was being punished for lying to the captain about being sixteen. If he got down alive he'd tell him what his real age was.

Would they just let him stay up there until there was no strength left in his arms and legs? He'd fall from the sky like a shot bird, dying like the *bukra* boy.

Would they let him stay up there when it turned night?

The only sounds came from the wind's whisper on the sails and the song of it on the lines and stays, and the creaking of the blocks. He could not hear his heartbeat but felt the drumming in his chest. He ground his teeth and clung on.

He had no way of telling time, but it seemed that almost an hour passed; he was still stuck like a weak, sick fly. The sun was lowering and the smell of fish frying from Thomas's galley began to rise up the mast. Yet Timothy could not bring himself to yell, "Come git me downg, pleese come git me downg . . ."

After a while he heard Thomas summoning the crew to eat and knew that the captain and Mr. Tanner had gone below for their meals. Maybe Horace was no longer manning the helm.

They were ignoring him as the sinking sun slanted along the mizzen skysail, brushing it with gold.

He looked up at his goal, the crosstrees above the foot of the mizzen royal, and tried to unlock his fingers from the rung above and move a leg at the same time. He swallowed and set his teeth but his body parts still didn't work. They were paralyzed.

He clung to the ratlines when the sun went down, turning the sea gray. The sails became shadowy. The breeze took on a chill edge. He glanced toward the stern of the *Theismann* and saw a wide path of white water that would soon turn light yellow as the sun set. He now knew the crew planned to let him stay on the shroud rungs all night if he chose to do that. Die if he might.

Just before total darkness he felt a swaying of the ladder ropes beneath him and heard a voice say, "Move on up to de crosstrees, Timothy. One step at a time."

Then Horace Simpson touched his ankle and said, "One step at a time an' go on up, boy."

Timothy felt his hands unlock and strength came back to his knees, and he reached for the next rung.

Horace talked the whole sixty feet up to the mizzen crosstrees, saying it wasn't any disgrace to freeze up there the first time you did it; saying Luther had bet him a quarter the boy'd either stay up there all night or fall out like the last one. Horace said they'd wait up there until moonshine. There was always a fine view on a moonlit night.

Sitting on the narrow platform waiting for the moon, feet dangling, Timothy confessed to Horace that he was only fourteen.

"Don' tell no one."

"Not eben de coptin?"

"Not no one. More man you are de longer yuh live out here," said Horace.

Timothy realized Horace was right and decided to keep his mouth shut.

Horace said he'd spent almost fifty years at sea, working a topsail schooner out of Mobile on his first voyage in 1838, at the age of fourteen. He'd spent his plantation boyhood on the banks of the muddy Tombigbee, which joined the Alabama River and emptied into the sea at Mobile.

Timothy wondered why Horace hadn't become a captain or at least a mate in all his years at sea.

"Not many black mates an' no black captains on big ships like this one," Horace said.

"Luther's black."

"Only part. Makes a difference."

"Yuh were a slave boy?" Timothy asked. He could barely see Simpson's face in the early darkness.

"Uh-huh. Then a slave man, till Mr. Lincoln's time. So I don't get no chance to be a mate. But bein' on ships was better'n workin' cotton."

Perched high in the warm night, fear finally gone, Timothy told Horace about wanting to have his own schooner and run down the Windwards and Leewards with passengers and crew. That was his never-ending dream, he said.

Horace laughed softly and said he thought Timothy ought to learn how to sail before thinking of being a captain on his own vessel.

They descended from the mizzen crosstrees after moonrise, around ten o'clock. Luther Oisten had the watch and Phelps was on the helm.

Oisten said to Horace, "I owe yuh nothin'. Yuh helped him downg."

Horace said, "Nice night, bo'sun," as they headed for the fo'c'sle.

In his bunk as the *Theismann* tacked back and forth going southward toward Rio, Timothy wondered if the father he'd never known was anything like Horace Simpson.

Or was he like the cruel Bajan, Luther Oisten?

15

The Devil's Mouth

There was excitement in my father's voice as he said, "Guess where I've been most of the day?"

"Sightseeing," I said. My parents had just entered the hospital room. It was late afternoon.

"Nope, I've been at the Hydrographic Office branch downtown. Got some navigation charts and a sailing direction book for the Caribbean."

He put them down on my lap.

My mother asked how I was. Her tone was quiet and sad.

"Okay," I said. "Fine."

Dr. Pohl would operate in the morning, but I was trying not to think about it.

I knew she was still hoping I'd change my mind; that my father would finally agree with her; that we could all tell the doctor, at the last moment, "No, thanks."

My father said, "I found all those places you said

Timothy talked about, and more. Here, let me read what the sailing directions say about Roncador . . ."

I heard him thumbing pages.

"'Roncador Bank—(13° 34' north latitude, longitude 80° 04' west)—lies seventy-five miles east-northeast of Isla Providencia. This very steep-to bank is about seven miles long and three and a half miles wide. Roncador Cay, composed of sand and blocks of coral, lies on the north part of the bank and is about thirteen feet high. The bank is fairly well covered with reefs, drying sand banks and coral heads . . .'"

I tried to picture it. "Does the book talk about Serrana Bank?"

"Yep, says it's a dangerous shoal area about forty-four miles north-northeast of Roncador . . ."

"Quita Sueño?"

"That one, too. 'Lies with its south end about thirty-nine miles north-northeast of Isla de Providencia and is very steep-to and dangerous. Great caution should be exercised by vessels passing east of Quita Sueño as the current sets strongly to the west . . .'"

"How about Serranilla?" Timothy had mentioned that one, and so had Captain Murry.

"'Lies seventy-eight miles north-northeast of Serrana Bank, twenty-four miles long, twenty miles wide, and very steep-to.'"

"Steep-to means the coral rises sharply?"

"Yep."

Somewhere around those cays and banks and shoals was Timothy's cay, our cay.

"I wish you could see this chart, Phillip. You will! Anyway, there are cays, banks, and shoals all over the place, and anyone who has sailed back in there will tell you not half are marked. It'll be like going through a minefield."

That's what both Timothy and Captain Murry had said.

Mother said, "I think I'll take a walk."

My father paused, probably looking at her as she went out the door. He started again, slowly, "Anyway, I talked to a guy in the company shipping office who's taken small tankers into both Bluefields and Puerto Cabezas, in Nicaragua, navigating right through those waters. He said they're awful, full of wrecks . . ."

"Captain Murry also said that . . ."

"So what we'll do is charter a sloop, maybe twenty-four, twenty-five feet, not much draft, and sail it straight to Catalina Harbor in Providencia Island, which belongs to Colombia, and hire a turtle fisherman to guide us to the Devil's Mouth. Panama to Providencia looks to be about two-fifty, two-seventy-five miles. How does that sound?"

"Sounds great," I said. *Would I be alive?*

"The guy in Curaçao said the turtlemen know those waters like no one else. Better to play it safe."

I nodded.

"When we get there, we'll anchor as close as we can, then you'll dive overboard and swim in. And if it's the right cay, I'll come in and you can show me around. Show me the palm trees you climbed, show me the hut if it's still there, the reef where you fished, Timothy's grave . . ."

"When can we do it?" I asked, fighting back tears.

"Next spring. The rainy season begins in May and the sailing directions say the northeasters blow from mid-June until early November; seas get rougher . . ."

I knew exactly why he was talking so much about going: to give me hope.

"I'll borrow a sextant and brush up on my navigation this winter," he said.

Would I be alive this winter? Would I be able to see this winter?

"We have to plan ahead."

He'd been an ocean sailor when he was younger. He sailed a twenty-two-foot cutter to Bermuda by himself when he was twenty-eight, before he married my mother.

I tried to think only of seeking out the cay and of what fun that would be.

"I'm looking at the chart now. Going to Providencia, until we get into the area of Cayos de Albuquerque, Cayo Bolivar, and San Andres Island, there shouldn't be any problems. Plenty of deep water all the way from the canal entrance."

Dr. Pohl said he was going to cut a window in my skull.

"How long will it take us to get to Providencia?"

"Oh, at five knots, let's say . . . three days—if we get fair winds—four days, at most . . ."

Dr. Pohl said there'd be seizures, minor ones but maybe major ones, too.

"Then we stay there how long?"

"Just long enough to hire a guide."

Dr. Pohl lost one patient on the operating table.

"Then from Providencia to the cay, how long?"

"Oh, another two days, if we're lucky. Maybe the turtlemen will know exactly where it is . . ."

Another patient was brain damaged.

A ticking in my stomach had begun. Much as I tried

not to, I was still thinking about tomorrow. I tried to clear my mind of the operating table and the ether smell and the gigli saw, but couldn't. My hands began to shake and I was ready to yell out, "I'll stay blind!" when my mother returned.

She said, "I saw Dr. Pohl in the hall, and he said he thought everything would go well tomorrow."

He'd said that to me this morning.

I said, "Could I please have a drink of water?"

I hated to have to ask someone for something so simple. But I'd already knocked two glasses off the bedside table by reaching for them.

She put the straw to my lips and said, "It's really pretty outside and not too hot." It had rained during the night. "Would you like to take a walk, Phillip?"

I said, "Okay." Maybe that would help. "The nurse said she put my shoes in the closet." I'd been in the room twenty-four hours and didn't know where the closet was. It seemed that every ten seconds, in every way, I was reminded that I was blind.

With my parents on either side, my father's hand lightly on my arm, guiding me, we left the hospital and walked a long way. The afternoon sun warmed my face and traffic noises rose and fell beside us. The exhaust fumes were bitter. Yet I didn't mind the sounds or the fumes. I welcomed all of them. I might never feel the sun again, hear the cars, smell the vapors. Suddenly, fear of the operation returned.

I tripped and fell, then tried to laugh it off.

––––––

Back in the room, we didn't talk very much. There didn't seem to be anything else to say.

I could smell food, hear the dinner carts out in the hallway, but knew there'd be no food for me tonight. Another reminder of tomorrow.

Just before visiting hours were over, the night nurse came in and said, without thinking, "It's going to be another beautiful sunset tonight."

At that moment, I knew for certain I had no choice. I had to go ahead with the operation. There were sunsets and sunrises I wanted to see. And cays.

My parents stood by my bed, holding hands with me, and it was my mother who said, "We love you very much, Phillip, and have great faith in you and in Dr. Pohl." She bent over and kissed me, saying, "We'll go up in the Empire State Building . . ."

My father said, "We'll need your eyes to spot those coral heads on the way to Providencia . . ."

He squeezed my hand until it hurt.

Those might be the last words I ever heard from them.

16

The Squall

APRIL 1886—Under full sail, the *Gertrude Theismann* was far out in the Atlantic, roughly 250 miles off Trinidad and Tobago, at the tip of South America, when the weather turned ugly. In early afternoon, heavy sooty clouds filled with electricity swept in from the east and claps of thunder echoed in the distance.

Timothy didn't need to be told that a storm was approaching after ten days of fair winds and gentle seas. He could see it and smell it. The air had suddenly freshened and chilled. The taut halyards and shrouds had begun to vibrate and sing. He felt a throb of excitement. He'd never been at sea in a storm.

Luther yelled, "Clear de topside!"

Stow anything loose that might slide or whip around. Check lashings. Loose gear could mean broken legs or worse.

Timothy stowed his holystone, the soft sandstone block he'd been grinding over the wooden deck several hours a day for a week, and then joined Horace Simpson. They tightened the straps on a couple of empty barrels used to catch rainwater.

Then the cold-edged wind began to screech and Mr. Tanner shouted orders to furl the royals, crojack, and flying jib. Lower and gather them in.

Timothy's heart beat faster.

The flying jib and crojack, the fore and aft lower sails, could be easily furled. The royals meant going high up the mast.

Timothy eyed them, those rectangles of canvas bellied out three-quarters the way up. He eyed the ratlines. Fear came back in a hot rush, shortening his breath.

As rain attacked in bursts, squall seas mounting, Timothy hesitated and Luther singled him out. "Lay aloft an' furl, you damn nigra boy . . ." His eyes matched the lightning, full of meanness.

This time the climb wasn't to test courage. This time there'd be no cowardly moment in which to cling to the ratlines, give way to the height or to the roar of the storm, plead silently for help.

Horace shouted, "Climb ahead o' me!" and shoved Timothy to join Luther and the others running across the slick deck toward the foremast. Salt spray sheeted over them. The ship had begun to heave and roll, slanting over the waves, heeling to port under the full spread of her sails. Those sails had to be reduced or they could be torn away.

For the second time in ten days, Timothy was going up a tall mast. This time rain spattered him, wind grabbed at him. Heart slamming, his hands grasped the ratlines as the sailor above him left them. He made his legs move up.

Over the storm's fury, he heard Horace shout, "Remember what I tol' you! . . ."

When you get out on the yard, lay your belly over it, let the footrope take your weight; keep the middle of your soles on the rope. Don't step, slide your feet along.

The footropes were about four feet below the yards. Below that was empty air, then the deck or roaring seas. Fall and die! Above were churning clouds.

Wishing he'd never seen a ship, wishing he were safe at home in Back o' All, Timothy climbed.

Horace kept shouting, "Keep goin', keep goin'! . . ." Then, "Go to starboard," as they reached the fore-royal's yard.

A rope less than an inch thick was the only thing between Timothy's soles and certain death 165 feet below. He wanted to close his eyes but didn't dare.

Moving around him, Horace shouted, "Come on out, yuh doin' fine!"

Timothy found it hard to breathe but forced himself to follow. He glanced over his shoulder and saw Luther grinning at him, coming his way. The grin said, *Meet Ol' Debbil Wind.*

In a moment, edging along the spar, separated from both Horace and Luther by seven or eight feet and sandwiched between them, Timothy found himself pulling at the leech lines to draw the wet canvas in. Leg and arm muscles straining, he soon realized he was almost as strong as the Bajan. There was no pause for fear. He didn't look down or up, just at the folds of the heavy, water-soaked canvas. *Gather them in; tie them off.*

Twice more, he went aloft, each time as scary as the

first. His feet slipped off the soaked mainroyal-yard
footrope, causing a suck of breath, causing his stomach
to drop like a cliff boulder. But his belly was firmly
across the spar, as Horace had instructed, and his hands
firmly clutched sail. A few seconds later he regained
footing and kept pulling.

After the sails had been furled, he collapsed on his
hands and knees on deck near the mizzenmast, as if he
were praying, his whole body trembling. Though the
squall wind had lessened, rain was still pelting down.

A moment later he raised his head and saw brown
feet in front of him. He looked upward into the bleak
face of Luther Oisten. "Lay aloft, nigra boy," said Luther. "Check de ties on de mainroyal."

It was unnecessary, everyone knew. Those ties would
hold even if the wind blew for three days. For three
weeks.

Timothy glanced at Horace, who was standing
nearby.

Horace was staring at the Bajan and seemed ready to
speak. Even to fight him. But an order was an order.

Horace finally looked back at Timothy and mur-
mured, "Do it." *Don't cross the bo'sun. Show him! Show
him, dammit.*

Luther smiled at Horace. "Yuh dis boy's keeper?"

Horace nodded. "In a way."

Meanwhile, Timothy was headed for the mainmast
shrouds, hoping there was enough strength still left
in his arms and legs to get him up and down the ratlines.

Captain Roberts and Mr. Tanner stood impassively,
just watching. After all, the captain had ordered the Bajan to train the boy.

When Timothy finally returned to the deck, exhausted, he hated Luther Oisten as much as he feared him. But Horace said quietly, "Yuh won."

He could climb and sail with the best of them, though he was only fourteen.

17

My Bald Head

At about eight o'clock, after my parents had gone back to the Commodore, an orderly came into the room to shave my head.

"My name is Harold," he said. "I'll be givin' you a free haircut. First I'll use the clippers, then a razor."

"On my whole head?"

"Yep."

"Why do you have to do that?"

"So no germs can get in during the surgery. Doctor's orders."

He asked me to sit on a chair, and soon the hair clipper buzzed. I knew I'd look funny if and when I ever saw myself. Completely bald.

Harold asked, "What kinda operation you gonna have?"

"There's a malformation on my optic nerve. Dr. Pohl is going to try and relieve the pressure. Then I can see again." Hopefully.

"Never heard any complaints about him," said Harold.

"He's supposed to be world famous," I said.

"That I didn't know," Harold said, as the buzzing stopped. Cut hair had fallen over my face and he brushed it off. "Now I'm going to put some shaving cream over your head. I want you to hold very still."

He said he had a straight razor, then he laughed. "You got to hold still 'less you want the surgery to begin tonight."

I felt the warm cream, then the sharp blade as he pulled it over my skull. It tickled more than hurt.

"Oops," he said.

I'd felt that cut.

"I nicked you. Shame on me! Jus' hold still."

Before he finished and wiped my skull clean, I heard a female voice. "Hi, I'm Dr. Leonard." Her hand touched mine. I could smell her perfume. "I'm your anesthesiologist. I'll be putting you to sleep in the morning."

Harold said, "And she does it right! . . . You can get back on your bed now." He said, "Good luck," and departed.

I ran my hand over my head. It felt like a bowling ball. I was almost glad I couldn't see myself.

As I climbed back on the bed, Dr. Leonard said, "You're the talk of the hospital. We've never had a castaway patient. You're a live Robinson Crusoe . . ."

That's what the newspapers and *Time* magazine had

said. *Life* had run a picture of me holding Stew Cat, walking off the *Sedgewick*.

"Mind if I sit here?" She sounded young.

"Fine."

"A lot of people, especially in this town, have wondered about being stranded on a tropical island. I'm almost envious."

"It was different," I said.

"I read that there was an old Negro with you. And a cat."

"Yes. Timothy died on the cay but my cat's in Curaçao."

"How long have you lived down there?"

"Two years, including the time on the cay."

"Some people have all the luck." Then she paused before saying, "Phillip, I'm going to do my very best to make you comfortable and keep you comfortable tomorrow. Mind if I ask you some questions? I've already talked to your parents."

"Ask whatever you want."

"Dr. Pohl said you had a tonsillectomy several years ago. Did you have any problems?"

"No, I just hated it when they put that mask over my face. The ether stinks."

"Yes, it does. I plan to have the nurse give you a sedative very early in the morning so that you'll be almost asleep when they wheel you out. Did you have any aftereffects?"

"I was sick to my stomach when I woke up. My throat hurt. They wouldn't let me have any water. Just an ice cube to suck on."

"That was because of surgery on your throat.

This time you can have all the water you can hold."

I nodded, then asked her about something that had been worrying me for almost a week, ever since the morning in Dr. Pohl's office. "Will I feel it or hear it when they start to drill?"

"I guarantee you won't. That's my job. You won't feel a thing," she said.

"How about when I wake up?"

"I'll be honest with you, Phillip. You won't feel very good. You'll feel very tired and weak. The back of your head will hurt."

"Do you think I'll be able to see?"

"Oh, I hope so," she said. "Dr. Pohl is one of the finest surgeons in the world. He works miracles."

I said, "I hope so, too."

She reached over and took my hand, squeezed it, then I heard her getting up. The chair squeaked on the linoleum floor. "The nurse will give you a sleeping pill at nine o'clock so you'll get a good night's rest, and I'll see you at six A.M."

She said, "Sleep well," and then her heels squeaked as she went away. I could always tell when someone was coming in and out by their heel squeaks. Her perfume lingered.

"Well, look at you," said the nurse when she came in at nine o'clock with the sleeping pill. "I like the shape of your head. No bumps."

"Do I look funny?" I asked, rubbing my palm back over my totally bald head.

"You look different. I tell any patient who has to be shaved that the hair starts growing back within two hours. It does. By the end of the week you'll feel stubble."

"Is that true?"

"Absolutely! Now, take this pill. . . ." She put it into my left hand, giving me a glass for the right one.

I swallowed the pill.

She fluffed my pillow and said, from habit, "Lights out."

I didn't argue.

Then she took my hand and held it a moment. "I go off at midnight, but I want to tell you not to worry. If there is one patient in this hospital who'll get the 'A' treatment, it's you. I'll be back on duty at four tomorrow afternoon."

She leaned over and kissed my forehead.

"G'night," she said, and squeaked away.

The hospital noises, softer now, floated in again. I remember thinking about that first hour of being blind. I was on the raft, of course, so frightened that I could hardly breathe. If your sight fades slowly, then I think you are finally prepared when all light is lost. When it is sudden, you panic.

Timothy held me tight during that first hour, I remembered. Real tight.

18

Home

APRIL 1890—Trace of a smile around his lips, eyes warm with memory, Timothy stood on the dew-wet deck of the SS *Bartolina* in the early-morning coolness as St. Thomas arose in the distance. The faint green dome of Crown Mountain welcomed him home. He'd been looking forward to this moment for four years.

After going to Rio, then to New York, on to France, then back to New York—a voyage of seven months— the *Gertrude Theismann* had made five more coffee runs to Rio and another to England, never coming near the Leeward Islands. He'd finally "jumped her," left without permission, a month ago.

As Tante Hannah would say, "De crab nebbah forget 'e hole."

Tante Hannah. Mr. Tanner, the chief mate of the *Theismann*, had been kind enough to write two short notes for Timothy to mail to Back o' All, telling her he was alive; that he thought of her constantly; that he missed her and loved her. There was no way of knowing whether or not she'd received them.

Main thing now, he was headed home at last, a "workaway" sailor, exchanging work with the *Bartolina*'s deck crew for passage from New York to St. Thomas. This was often done when a sailor had little or no money.

He'd changed. He knew he'd changed, in his body and in his head. After leaving the island as a boy, he was returning as a man of eighteen, more than six feet in height, body heavily muscled from days and nights of heaving on lines and grappling with sails, fair weather or storm.

He'd learned much aboard the *Theismann*, even from the Bajan. But now he swore that never again would he leave his own sea, the summery Caribbean, his gentle islands and cays. The two trips across the Atlantic had taught him about gales and snow and ice. From now on, he'd sail where palm trees grew and trade winds caressed, where the sky and the ocean stayed blue most of the time. He still didn't like shoes.

"Dere 'tis, my islan'," he said to a *bukra* sailor standing nearby him.

The early sun was lighting up Crown Mountain.

"I bin homesick foh *four* year. Feel de wahrm win' . . ." He tilted his head toward Crown Mountain, his smile increasing until it was as brilliant as the sun.

"Who are you going home to?" the sailor asked.

"My Tante Hannah, de womahn who raise me."

"No girlfriends?" the sailor asked.

Timothy laughed. "None dat I know of." Girls

hadn't been on his mind four years back. Going to sea had been about the only thing in his head. Maybe girls would enter his life now.

"You plan to stay ashore?"

He'd thought about that a lot. He thought he'd stay with Tante Hannah for a while, take up where he'd left off: go fishing with Wobert Avril, spend some time with Charlie Bottle, then find a job on an interisland schooner. Go down the Leewards and the Windwards.

First, though, was Tante Hannah. "Ah tink Ah'll be sittin' ashore foh a while."

Hidden under his mattress in crew's quarters were gifts for her from Rio, France, and England. In a leather sack tied to his waist were twenty-six gold dollars. Six would go to her; twenty would go to the Bank of Denmark, toward his own schooner. That dream was as much alive as it had been when he was twelve.

"Evah bin downg here?" Timothy asked, shifting his look to the sailor.

"No."

"Ah, go to Magen's Bay, jump into de wahrm wattah, den sit 'neath a coconut palm. Dat's whot I plan to do . . ."

Get his feet and bottom into warm sand again.

Thick black smoke coiled up from the stack of the *Bartolina*, the first steamship Timothy had ever boarded. Though it was steadier and sometimes faster than the *Theismann*, Timothy missed the quietness and cleanliness of the bark. The coal-burner's engine thudded and the iron hull shook. Another reason to return to sailing.

Breakfast call sounded an hour out of St. Thomas,

Crown Mountain growing closer with each turn of the propeller. Then the bo'sun, a *bukra* this time, kinder than the Bajan, issued orders to prepare the ship for entry to port.

Timothy's pulse quickened. It seemed even more than four years since he left the island.

Salt Cay and West Cay were in sight as the *Bartolina* steered southeast to round the tip of St. Thomas. Soon she'd round Turtledove Cay and Saba Island, then steer east until time to swing north and steam up the channel into the harbor.

Twenty minutes later he saw the powder magazine and gun batteries on the tip of Hassel Island. In the distance, on St. Thomas's shore, were Fort Christian and King's Wharf, where he'd spent those hours watching sailors and ships.

His excitement mounted as the ship put Flamingo Point, on Water Island, abeam. Now the route was a few hundred yards east of Hassel, and there was the *Glory* waiting off the port bow to help her into the West India Company berth in the harbor itself.

———

Within minutes after the *Bartolina* was tied up, Timothy trudged along the dirt road that circled the harbor, going westward along the waterfront toward Crown Bay. Slung across his back, a canvas bag that he'd sewed together on the *Theismann* held his few possessions. In his right hand, wrapped in oilcloth, were Tante Hannah's gifts—a dress and a red parasol from France, a hat from Rio, a bracelet from England. He couldn't wait to see her face as she looked at them, then tried on the hat.

They would talk for days, he thought, because Tante

Hannah had never left St. Thomas in all her life—not even to go to St. John or St. Croix. She knew no other island, and now he could tell her what was beyond the horizon and what had happened to him there.

He hurried his steps as he came closer to Back o' All and broke into a trot to go up the hill. Very little had changed on the waterfront and along the row of warehouses. Some of the same down-island schooners were in port but he didn't stop to say hello. He'd come back later.

Finally, he reached the top of the hill, expecting to see Tante Hannah out by the iron wash kettle, see *bukra* clothes on the line. He planned to sweep her off her feet, hug her, kiss her, tell her how much he'd missed her.

He slowed and then stopped. There was no kettle in the yard of her shack, no Tante Hannah stirring it, no clothes on the line. Someone was sitting on the doorstep, a woman—but she wasn't Tante Hannah. He'd never seen the woman before. Then he heard a baby crying, the sound coming from inside the shack. A baby in Tante Hannah's house?

Suddenly uneasiness turned to alarm as he stood there, staring at the thin-faced woman. She stared back. He took a few more steps, then asked, "Whe' be Hannah Gumbs?"

"Her lamp done went out." The young woman's eyes were remote.

"Don' fool wit' me," Timothy said angrily. Tante Hannah was strong and healthy.

"Her oil gone," said the woman, who looked to be in her twenties.

Timothy found it hard to breathe. "When?"

"Two year ago. Who yuh be?"

"Her son." Yes, he was her son, as much as there was a son anywhere on earth.

"Two year ago," the woman repeated.

"I don' believe yuh."

The woman shrugged. "She gone. We lib here . . ."

No one owned property in Back o' All. When someone died, it was fair game unless a relative moved in quickly. Quickly meant within hours.

Timothy turned his back and walked slowly toward Mama Geeches's, his feet leaden, pain crushing him from inside. Tears rolled down his cheeks.

It wasn't possible. Tante Hannah had never been sick.

A smell of incense drifted out of Mama Geeches's shack. She always lit it with candles, twenty or thirty of them burning even in daylight. Mama Geeches, when she wasn't on her feet, stayed atop an old hospital bed. Her customers sat beside it on a stool.

Dropping his sea bag, Timothy looked in. She was fully dressed but dozing, no matter that it was ten o'clock in the morning. Steeling himself in the doorway against the truth, he said sharply, "Mama Geeches, wake up."

Her eyes fluttered open and she squinted. "Who be yuh?"

"Timothy. Tante Hannah's son. Wher' be she?"

"Otha side she gone."

The other side. Timothy had never liked the word but had to know. "Dead?"

Mama Geeches nodded.

"How?"

"Heart done gib out. She jus' dropped in de yard doin' wash foh de *bukra* . . ."

Timothy nodded and picked up the sea bag to walk slowly away from Back o' All.

The same strong smell of sewer and cooking over open fires was in the air. The shantytown looked even poorer after four years.

He went to the very edge of it, then sat down and sobbed.

Charlie Bottle said, "She buried on Estate Alborg, near her mama and papa . . ."

Charlie said he made her pineboard coffin himself and then used his hay cart to transport her from Back o' All to the estate. Because she was a weedwoman, almost everyone in shantytown turned out for the procession in their finest. The procession was a quarter-mile long, he said.

"Ah kept her 'ead pointed wes'."

That meant her feet were toward the donkey's tail as it drew the cart. Head to the east invited Loupgarau and Soucayant and the *jumbis* to walk beside the procession.

Timothy nodded. He was still in shock. He'd done a terrible thing. He'd stayed away too long. He'd thought Tante Hannah would never die.

"Yuh lookin' good," said Charlie Bottle. "Yuh growed up."

Timothy nodded, then said to Charlie Bottle that he'd see him later. He gave Charlie the gifts he'd bought for Tante Hannah, saying, "Fo' yuh womahn."

He wanted to go to Estate Alborg and pay his respects.

On the way he picked some red hibiscus, Tante Hannah's favorite flower, and placed them on her grave, staying by it for more than an hour.

Then he returned to Charlie Bottle's and asked about Wobert Avril. He thought he'd like to go fishing with Wobert in the morning, clear his mind.

"He done gone otha side, too," said Charlie.

Timothy's four years away from home had been costly.

He stayed the night with Charlie and then in the morning went down to King's Wharf to find work on an interisland schooner and pursue his dream of having his own boat.

EDMOND H. TAVEIRNE
MIDDLE SCHOOL
LEARNING CENTER
34699 N. Highway 12
Ingleside, IL 60041

WITHDRAWN

19

The Operating Room

A voice, awakening me, said, "I have a pill for you."

"What time is it?" I asked.

"Five o'clock."

"Do they always operate this early?"

"Only on special people. Just one sip of water."

I swallowed the pill.

"Do you need to go to the johnny?"

I said yes and got out of bed. I was still drowsy from the pill last night and stumbled.

I'm not too sure of what happened in the next hours, but I remember being rolled onto a bed with wheels, then going on an elevator to another floor and down a long hall, finally through the doors of the operating room. I was holding Timothy's knife. Somewhere along the way Dr. Leonard had joined me. I remember her voice as she bent over me.

As things got hazy, I remembered deciding that I'd dream of the cay while they bored those holes and cut that oblong window into my skull. Just before I faded away I saw Timothy standing against one wall, a wide smile on his face.

He said, "Don' warry, Phill-eep, yuh in safe hans."

20

Captain

JULY 1916—Timothy, having just returned from three years in Panama, $596 richer from digging canal mud with a pick and shovel and a mule drag team, found Charlie Bottle beneath the sizzling tin roof of Market Square, between Kronprindsen's Gade and Torve Strade. He was playing checkers.

Charlie, toothless as a day-old chipmunk, thinning hair as white as the inside of a turnip, had turned eighty the year past. He soon became aware that Timothy was standing there two feet away and looked up, smiling a little. "Fevah din't getcha, huh?" That was his only greeting.

Malaria had sent several hundred Virgin Island canal workers to early graves over in Panama. Timothy smiled back at his old friend and shook his head. "'Tween me an' de muskitas, dey lost." Barely. He'd almost died over there from the high jungle fever. He bent down to hug Charlie Bottle, who was as near to a father as Timothy ever had.

In the shade of the open-air market stalls a half-dozen checkerboards were occupied by men more or less Charlie's age. They gathered daily to talk and smoke and see who could be best at checkers. Vegetables, fruit, and fish were laid out on wooden tables nearby; chattering women guarded them, shooing flies. July heat had turned Charlotte Amalie into a humid furnace.

Charlie introduced his checker partner. "Mistah Alonzo Lockhart . . ." He looked to be as old as Charlie, shiny bald head tucked down between his shoulder blades.

Timothy didn't remember Mr. Lockhart.

" 'E from Tortola," Charlie explained. "One o' dem British boys runnin' from 'e wife." Charlie cackled, his gums showing.

It was good to see Charlie Bottle again. Timothy hadn't been sure he'd still be alive. Most of the older people from his boyhood were gone. And three more years away from St. Thomas hadn't helped that situation. Before going to Panama, he'd crewed on down-island schooners, living aboard them to save money.

"How ol' yuh now, boy?" Charlie asked, squinting up, frowning.

"Forty-sumthin'," Timothy replied, sitting down on the stone wall beside the market walkway. "Pushin' fifty, ah guess . . ." But he was still lean, his forearm muscles looking as hard as the stone on which he sat. Even his neck was heavily muscled. Pick-and-shovel work.

"Now yuh bock, time yuh settle down," Charlie advised. "Git yuhself a womahn, chillun . . ."

Timothy made a laughing noise deep in his throat. Men who went to sea didn't make good husbands, and to sea was where he intended to go.

Alonzo Lockhart made three quick jumps with his red piece, and Charlie, having paid more attention to Timothy than to the game, howled in protest.

Timothy said, "Charlie, 'tween whot Ah got in d' bank 'ere an whot Ah made in Panama, Ah finally got enuff to buy me a boat."

Charlie regarded Timothy with surprise and whistled softly. "Mahn, yuh gotta fortun', a fortun'! Buy sum cows, Ah say. Don' buy no boat." Charlie had sold his twenty-cow dairy when gathering hay had become too much for him.

Timothy thought he could buy a good schooner or sloop for $800. Over the years, he'd saved up $906. He'd use the $106 to live on until he could get cargoes and passengers, buy rice and beans, get her shipshape.

"Ah'm buyin' a boat."

Charlie shook his head. "Yuh stubborn as dat ol' donkey Ah buried las' year. 'E died sayin' no."

Timothy nodded, smiling widely. Maybe he was donkey stubborn. It had taken him almost thirty years to gather the money. But he knew there were black men who didn't have ten *kroner* in the bank. "Yuh 'bout to look at Coptin Timothy . . ."

"Don' hang yuh *cattacoo* too high," said Charlie, eyeing Timothy.

Charlie was beginning to sound like Tante Hannah, God bless her. Well, Timothy wasn't hanging his basket too high. He'd been going to sea thirty years and could sail on any ship afloat. "Finish yuh game an Ah'll buy yuh a rhum. Ah need to talk, Charlie . . ."

Glancing down at the board, Charlie said, "Dat won't be too long. . . ." Only two of his checkers remained.

Mr. Lockhart made his last jump and Charlie said, "A good marnin' to yuh," and rose up.

A moment later, Timothy walked slowly up sandy Torve Strade beside the old man, Charlie using his cane to maintain balance.

Timothy needed Charlie Bottle to make his deal. Charlie could read and write, somewhat, taught by a woman from the Lutheran Church long ago. He was also good at figures. They soon sat down for a glass of rum.

The next day, Timothy said to Charlie Bottle, "Das 'er," pointing to a two-masted wooden-hulled schooner riding at anchor in Vessup Bay, on the east end of the island. A For Sale sign was tacked at the base of her foremast. Her name was *Tessie Crabb*, built in Grenada.

Salt streaks had turned her white paint brownish in places, and she needed work. But she looked sound. Of course, Timothy couldn't tell until he careened her at low tide and looked for worms. She was 49.6 feet long and 15.7 in breadth. She belonged to the widow Tessie Crabb, wife of the late Captain Elias Crabb. She'd been at anchor for almost a year. Her bottom was dirty.

"How much she want?" Charlie Bottle asked.

They were standing on the beach at Vessup.

"A t'ousand," Timothy replied, eyes narrowed against the glare of the sun staring at the *Tessie Crabb*. "More'n Ah wanted to pay."

"A t'ousand?" Charlie repeated, as if there wasn't that much money in the whole of St. Thomas.

"But de bod part is, she lettin' de Bonk o' Denmark sell it, 'cause she owe de Bonk two hun'red. Coptin Crabb left 'er wit dat debt . . ."

Charlie Bottle blinked and frowned. "An' yuh want me to talk to de bonk?"

"Ah want yuh to lend me two hun'red dollar, den sit by me when I talk to de bonk."

"Yoh din't say dis yesterday."

"Ah'm sayin' it today."

Charlie Bottle stared at Timothy. "Two hun'red? Dat is a lot o' money. How yuh gonna pay me bock?"

"A lil' at a time," Timothy said. "Mebbe ten a mont', soon's I start gittin' cargo an' passengers."

Charlie looked back at the schooner. "S'pose she got rotten sails?"

"Dem sails number-four duckcloth, good as new."

"S'pose dat hull rotten," Charlie said.

"Ah'm gonna careen 'er tomorrow, look fer rot an' worm holes . . ."

Charlie kept looking at the *Tessie Crabb*. "S'pose dem frames rotten."

"Frames made o' white oak. Last a hun'red years, less I pile 'er up on a reef."

"Riggin'?" said Charlie, trying to find an excuse.

"Roeblin's bes' wire."

Charlie blew a breath out. "Caulkin'?" That kept her from leaking.

"Two threads cotton, five oakum, hawsed well bock an' payed wit pitch."

"How yuh know so much, Timothy?" Charlie snorted.

Timothy laughed long and hard. "'Cause ah bin goin' to sea since I was fo'teen. Yuh memory give out, Charlie."

Charlie shook his head. "All right. Yuh 'ave to sign me a paper. Yuh pay bock fifteen percent interest."

Timothy shrugged. He had no idea what 15 percent interest would be. It didn't matter. So long as the hull was sound, he wanted this schooner to fulfill his dream.

On August 14, 1916, the former *Tessie Crabb*, now renamed *Hannah Gumbs* (home port, St. Thomas, Virgin Islands) put out to sea past Rupert Rock and Muhlenfels Point, turning south off Buck Island, with eight passengers and a mixed cargo bound for St. Johns, Antigua.

It would be a typical voyage. One lady was taking bags of seed, fertilizer, thread, soap, cotton materials, and live chickens, all for sale on Antigua. On the return trip, Timothy knew he'd have two tons of charcoal, the same of firewood; then some road oil and fresh fruits.

Standing at her wheel near the taffrail, the rail over her stern, steering her, was Timothy, a huge grin on his face. On his head was a cap, gift of Charlie Bottle. The gold-thread letters said *Captain*.

21

Awakening

I seemed to be swimming through warm cotton as I slowly woke up. Nearby voices sounded as if they were coming out of a tunnel. Tongue thick, mouth parched, I could still smell the ether. The back of my head hurt and I was very tired. But I knew I was alive. I hadn't died on the operating table.

Mother's voice said, "Phillip, you're okay. It's all over." Her hand clutched mine.

"The doctor said it went fine. They repaired all the veins." My father's voice.

They told me later that my first words were, "Where is Timothy?"

Then I drifted back into the warm cotton for a while, voices fading out as I floated away again. I wanted to float away, and I remember doing that several times, like I was surfacing, then sinking again.

Finally, my body seemed to stay put in that room, and I asked what time it was.

"Nine-twenty-five," my father said.

"In the morning?"

"No, it's night," Mother said. "You came out of the operating room at four-fifteen this afternoon."

"I still can't see," I said, my voice sounding feeble.

"Remember, the doctor told you it might take several weeks. The nerves have to heal," my father said.

I tried to nod my head but realized it was strapped down so that my cheek was against the bed sheet. "Why is my head this way?"

"So you don't put pressure on the back of it," another voice said. "I'm Eileen, your special nurse."

I was thirsty and asked for water. Someone put a straw into my mouth.

I'd never felt so weak in all my life.

I drifted off again, not wanting to talk.

The next time I woke up I heard the voice of another stranger asking if I needed anything. She said she was Helen, another special nurse staying in the room with me. I asked what time it was.

"Just past midnight."

I'd been on the table ten hours, she said.

I stayed awake a little longer, then went back into that warm place where I was hiding. Later, Eileen told me that was a natural reaction to the surgery and to spending a long time under ether.

I think I slept up to the time a strong hand was squeezing mine and the gruff voice of Dr. Pohl was saying, "Good morning. I don't know about you, but

I've got to go down to the cafeteria and have my breakfast. How do you feel?"

It took a moment to answer him. "Like I hit a rock wall."

"You did, but your temperature is normal, blood pressure is normal. You're doing fine so far. I'm going to shine a light in your eyes. Tell me what you see . . ."

I waited.

"See anything?"

"Nothing."

"That's okay. I didn't expect a miracle. Give it time . . ." He gave me a slap on the leg and said, "I'll come by again late this afternoon. Meanwhile, get some food in your belly."

———————

Two days later Dr. Pohl said, "The incision is healing nicely. No sign of infection." He'd lifted the bandage on the back of my head and the nurse was standing by to put another fresh one on. "You're doing fine."

The next six days were the longest in my life. I kept hoping I'd see light of some kind, even dim light, but that darkness I'd lived in since April showed no signs of lifting.

Each day the doctor would come in and make his test with the tiny flashlight, and each time my answer was the same. He wasn't much comfort. He remained gruff and once said, "I don't try to win friends around here. I said I didn't guarantee you'd see again. Let nature work."

I cried several times after he left, giving up hope.

My parents came twice a day to read to me and tell

me what they'd been doing outside. They tried to keep my spirits up but we ran out of things to talk about. Although Dr. Pohl had said it might take two weeks to notice any results, I kept thinking the operation had failed. I wouldn't go through it again.

22

Jennifer

AUGUST 1928—Timothy had returned to St. Thomas from Porto Rico aboard the *Hannah Gumbs* with a cargo of freight, six grunting breeder hogs, and five passengers, and he was unloading at the King's Wharf when Mrs. Josiah Redd walked up to him and said, "De coptin done bus 's rope . . ." Her husband had died.

The frail gray-haired woman in a wide white hat stood on the wharf midships of the *Hannah Gumbs*, her face sad and grave.

"Ah'm sorry to hear dat. Josiah was a good mahn," Timothy said, his own face suddenly sad and grave. They'd been friends for years, had helped each other obtain cargo and passengers.

" 'E balmed in Anteega. De *Hettie Redd* still downg dere," she said. Her husband was embalmed in Antigua

130

and his schooner was still there. "Ah'd 'preciate veree much yuh fetch 'em home."

Timothy did not hesitate in saying yes.

Antigua, a British possession, was some three hundred miles southeast, in the Leeward Islands, near Barbuda and St. Kitts. Timothy had sailed the *Hannah Gumbs* down there many times. Now he would have to lay her up for a few weeks and lose some income. But his long friendship with Captain Josiah required him to help Mrs. Redd. She smiled briefly, nodded, and moved off into the dockside traffic of horse carts and stevedore's handcarts.

He watched her go, wondering why he'd never taken a wife of his own. His hair was now as gray as hers. He thought he was in his late fifties, too late for marriage and children. He often wondered who would mourn for him when the flame in his own lamp flickered out.

The following Tuesday he boarded the Furness Withy Line ship *Cardiff* for the day-and-a-half voyage to Antigua. He hadn't sailed on a steamship since the *Bartolina*.

There were no docks at St. Johns, Antigua, and schooners had to anchor in the sheltered waters, as did steamships. Barges with great sweep oars took the cargoes between the anchorages and the warehouses.

Timothy spotted the *Hettie Redd* not long after the *Cardiff* passed through the narrow neck and entered the harbor. She was sturdy, a good vessel in a stormy seaway, Josiah had said.

As soon as immigration and customs cleared the

Cardiff, Timothy went ashore and headed directly to the funeral home. Though the man in the wooden box was an old friend, Timothy had to steel himself against certain misgivings about the voyage. It was bad luck to transport the dead on a wind-powered ship, he'd always heard. The spirits of the ocean breeze would become angry if they discovered what was in the box.

The papers were signed. Keeping his eyes away from the casket on the donkey cart, he walked beside it to the lightering wharf. The donkey threaded through a herd of goats in the jasmine-scented air. Smoke rose from the hills beyond the harbor as wood was burned to make charcoal.

After the box was off-loaded he made arrangements to take Josiah out to his beloved *Hettie Redd*, telling the boy who owned the rowboat to wait awhile. Then he walked to the corner of Market and St. Mary's, to the offices of Mohan Singh, shipping agents, to see if they had any cargo or passengers to be forwarded to St. Thomas.

"The cargo is aboard and you'll have four passengers," said one of the Singh sons, a handsome East Indian. "When will you sail?"

"Sooner de bettah," Timothy replied. The hurricane season had begun in July, though none had swept up the Antilles as yet. But the stillness of the early September air made him uneasy. Flags hung limp. Palm fronds were silent.

"Tomorrow morning?" Shri Singh asked.

Timothy nodded.

"I'll see to it that your passengers are on board by eight o'clock."

Timothy nodded again. "Anyting 'bout de wedder?"

Ships sometimes sent messages by cable or radio to report tropical disturbances. Shri shook his head and smiled. "But it is hot, isn't it?"

Timothy agreed. Very hot.

As he left Mohan Singh he had an ominous feeling. The face of the sea had changed during the night, he thought. The long rollers were smooth as glass.

He signed for the cargo that had already been put in the *Redd* and returned to the lightering wharf to be rowed out to the schooner with Josiah in his box. The harbor was active this day, and Timothy looked from ship to ship, trying to ignore the casket.

Soon the boat bumped up against the white hull, Timothy shouting to deckhands Alfonso Jarvis and Wilmer Lockett to come and help take Josiah aboard.

Alfonso said, "Yuh be coptin an' take us home?"

Timothy frowned up at the young black sailor. "Why yuh tink Ah'm here?" He knew these boys from Charlotte Amalie. They were all right. Captain Redd wouldn't have allowed fools to work his deck.

The passengers came aboard just before eight in the morning, Alfonso and Wilmer taking their luggage to the cabin space below. There were six bunks down there, but the ventilation was the same as sleeping in a closet. Except in heavy rain, straw mats on deck offered cool breezes and a view of the stars.

The Negro passengers were John Dews and Dr. O. W. Bird, going to visit relatives in the British Virgins. The white passengers were merchant Oliver Rankin and his ten-year-old daughter, Jennifer. All were British subjects.

Rankin said, "We could have gone on a steamer but I wanted my daughter to have a voyage under sail."

Jennifer was a fair-skinned, green-eyed redhead. Timothy said to her, "Bes' yuh stay in de shade."

Dr. Bird advised the girl, "Put some vegetable oil on your face and arms."

"I have a parasol," Jennifer said.

"Dis sun'll roas' right through dat silk," Timothy said.

"Listen to them," her father said.

The *Hettie Redd* swung around while Alfonso and Wilmer "walked" the capstan to heave in the anchor. Timothy stood at the helm, eyeing the sails, then moved it a few spokes as Alfonso shouted, "Ankar home . . . ," and the schooner got underway. There was barely enough wind for steerage.

As she passed slowly through the draw, Timothy, unable to shake off the ominous feeling, searched the heavens for cirrus clouds. They were usually the first signs of a hurricane. If a tempest was on its way, they would stretch in bands and gradually thicken to cirro-stratus, rising to great heights.

Timothy knew the cirrus as "cat's tails," slender, wavy parallel lines penciled in white on the blue sky. When the fine threads of the cirrus appeared to be blown or brushed backward at one end, toward the roof of the sky, the wind would sooner or later veer around to that point. He'd seen it happen.

The course was west-by-north, skirting the islands of Nevis, St. Kitts, Sint Eustatius, and Saba, finally angling by Virgin Gorda and on into St. Thomas.

By midafternoon, the breeze was as dead as Captain

Josiah. The schooner drifted helplessly about fifteen miles off Antigua, her sails not even flapping. The long swells were as slick as the silk on Jennifer's parasol. The heat bore down on the *Hettie Redd*. Timothy sat on a fruit box by the helm and studied the barometer, which measured air pressure. It was abnormally high.

He was uneasy.

At sundown, there was a threatening, flaming red border across the west horizon, and through the thin veils of cirrus clouds, a solar halo could be seen. Timothy studied it while the *Hettie Redd* drifted.

Alfonso, the oldest deckhand, asked, "We gonna git de tempis?" He asked it quietly so the passengers couldn't hear.

Timothy nodded.

The *Cardiff* scurried by them, smoking furiously from her stack. "Runnin' from de starm," Timothy observed. Her captain didn't want to be caught in port and wrecked on shore. Maybe he'd received a radio warning.

"Isn't it a lovely sunset?" said Jennifer, who'd come aft to stand beside Timothy.

Turning to look at her, he replied, slowly, "Ah bes' 'ave it clear."

"You've been going to sea a long while?" she said.

"Mos' o' my life. More dan forty years . . ."

"I think I'd like to become a sailor and sail all the seas. Such adventure. But girls aren't allowed to be sailors. I say, why not, Captain Timothy?"

He examined her. Her skin was like those jars they called porcelain. She was so serious. If he was a *bukra* and had a daughter, he'd like her to be a Jennifer Rankin. He laughed softly. " 'Tis a 'ard life out 'ere. Dere days when de sea is calm an' pretty. Den days when she go wil' an' de waves turn white, high as dat mas'. Dose days 'tis no place foh mahn or womahn . . ."

———

The horizon flamed again for a few minutes at dawn. As the bowl of the sky lightened, Timothy, who had only dozed during the hot, still night, staying by the helm, saw that the cat's tail clouds, now stretching in bands across the sky, had begun to thicken and rise.

The barometer started to fall and a light easterly breeze rippled the long, oily swells that rolled as far as the eye could see. He estimated that the *Hettie Redd* had now drifted about twenty-five miles west and north of Antigua. If the hurricane gave him time he'd run west and duck into the lee of St. Kitts, knowing that its mountain towered up almost four thousand feet, providing some shelter from the wild wind.

Midmorning, when an arc of dense, dark clouds began to form at the point where the clouds converged, Oliver Rankin worriedly approached Timothy. "Are we in for a storm?"

"Yes, sirrah, Ah tink we are."

"Can't we return to Antigua?"

"Ah don't tink we 'ave de time. De win' be blowin' us west."

"You're responsible for our lives and safety, Captain," Rankin reminded him.

"Ah'll do all I can, sirrah," Timothy replied. He now realized he might have made a mistake leaving Antigua. While the *Hettie Redd* would risk being wrecked in the harbor, his passengers would have a chance at getting ashore safely. In open sea, their chances were considerably less.

Shortly before eleven, the barometer fell again and light rain sprinkled the ocean. The sun vanished and the air turned cool. At first, the rising wind was light, filling the sails, and Timothy set a course due west as bluish black clouds swelled and spread. He ordered Alfonso and Wilmer to batten down the hatches and secure the deck.

For a moment, now that the *Hettie Redd* was moving again, he considered trying to reach Antigua, but he'd have to tack back and forth to do it. There wouldn't be enough time. He was committed to running before the storm.

Soon the barometer dropped as if it had no bottom and the black clouds began to race above the schooner. The rain became torrential. Timothy shouted, "Ebrybodee put on de life jackets!" Alfonso had brought them up from below and had rigged lifelines near the helm. He ordered the passengers to hang on to the lengths of rope.

The sails were dropped and secured. The *Hettie Redd* would run before the wind on bare masts. It was already blowing thirty or forty miles an hour, enough to send the hull forward without the canvas wings.

Just before noon, the edge of the hurricane finally caught the *Hettie Redd*. The wind shrieked, and mountainous waves, surging from the stern, drove the hull as if it were a tiny sliver of bark, sending it up walls of white-veined water. Then it staggered down into valleys, burying the bow, the sea washing waist deep back over the deck.

Timothy clung to the helm, trying to keep the

schooner bow first in the waves. He glanced at the huddled, drenched passengers and crew. They were holding desperately to the lifelines.

He couldn't see Dr. Bird. He shouted to Alfonso.

"Ovahboard," Alfonso shouted back.

Rankin's face was flour white. He was gripping the lifeline with one hand, holding Jennifer with the other.

For almost two hours, the *Redd* survived the giant gray seas that were towering over her stern, then lifting her with a mighty thrust to drop her into another huge hollow. Timothy had never seen such rage in the sea. As he watched helplessly, John Dews let go the lifeline, and though Wilmer tried to grab him as his body hung on the after rail for a few seconds, he tumbled into the water.

Finally, the *Hettie Redd* surrendered. A monster wave, racing down on her before she could struggle up from the last one, twisted the hull sideways and she turned turtle, masts pointing toward the bottom for a few seconds.

Her rigging entangled Timothy, Alfonso, Wilmer, and Oliver Rankin. Jennifer disappeared.

Timothy broke loose and fought back to the surface, seeing Jennifer floating nearby in her cork life jacket. He used all his strength to swim to her and wrap his arm around her. She was unconscious. He found the stub of a boom and hooked one arm over it, holding her with the other. They rode the huge seas.

Finally, she came to but did not speak. She just looked at him with those green eyes. They seemed to be asking, *Why did it happen to us? To me?* Her sodden red hair framed her face.

He shouted, "Hang on, hang on! . . ."

A few minutes later, the wooden box containing Captain Josiah Redd skidded down the hill of a wave near them. Timothy ducked from it, turning away. The spirits of the ocean breeze had gotten what they wanted.

For the next two hours, Timothy and Jennifer struggled in the ocean mountains, streaked with white spindrift; gasping in the hollows, rising to the crests where the wild wind tore off wave tops and made blinding, salty arrows out of them. Timothy knew Jennifer was swallowing water, and he could feel the strength leaving her. She'd closed her eyes, giving up. He shouted to her, again and again, "We'll lib, we'll lib! . . ." But there was no response.

The roaring wind slowed; then it ceased. Quiet descended and the clouds parted. The sun shone down brightly on the still-heaving, foam-licked gray seas. They were floating in the eye of the hurricane, and Timothy kept saying encouraging words to Jennifer even though he knew she was dead from exhaustion and terror. He also knew that the full fury of the storm, coming from the opposite direction, would likely start again within an hour. But he refused to give up the slight body he was holding.

A day later, Timothy, still holding Jennifer Rankin, washed ashore on the island of Nevis; he was the only survivor of the schooner *Hettie Redd*. Jennifer stared lifelessly at him as he dragged her up onto the beach. He knew he'd forever be haunted by that pretty face and those warm green eyes. He alone had made the decision, as captain, to leave the comparative safety of St. Johns Harbor. There were dark times ahead, day and night, when he would wish he'd drowned with Jennifer.

23

Trees

On the ninth day after surgery, just before noon, something strange occurred. I was alone in the room and suddenly saw clouds and trees, very distinctly. I screamed, "I can see, I can see!" and buzzed the nurse to tell her to call Dr. Pohl.

When she came into the room, I said, "I can see trees and clouds . . ."

"Where?"

"Right out there," I said, pointing.

"But you're not even looking out the window."

"I can see them," I insisted.

"The sky is blue, not a cloud in it, and we're too high up for you to see treetops . . ."

I couldn't believe her. "Is there something in the room that looks like clouds and trees? A painting, maybe?"

"Nothing on these walls. They're green. There's not a thing on them," she said.

"I tell you, I can see them."

"Okay. I'll put it on your chart. Dr. Pohl is in surgery," the nurse said.

In a few minutes, the clouds and trees disappeared and I broke into tears.

When my parents came in, after lunch, I asked them to look out the window and see if there were clouds and trees out there. "Fluffy white clouds and green trees," I said. "I saw them."

They were slow to answer. "Well, that's wonderful, Phillip," my father said. The tone of his voice said he felt something else: *alarm*.

Mother said, "You told the nurse?"

"She didn't believe me."

"Well, those are nice things to see," said my mother. Her tone said she might agree with the nurse. That the operation had affected my mind.

I got angry. "*I did see them!*"

"Do you see them now?" my father asked.

"No!" I shouted.

They stayed until late afternoon. We walked along the hallways for a while. I'd been on my feet for more than a week, went to the johnny by myself, even took showers by myself. This was my father's last visit. He was flying back to Curaçao that night on Pan Am. He kissed me and hugged me, saying he knew I'd have my sight back soon. But his voice was hollow.

About an hour later, I heard Dr. Pohl's voice in the hallway, then he came in. "What's going on in here? Miss Evans told me you were seeing things . . ."

I said I had seen things. "Nobody believes me, but I saw trees and clouds today."

He laughed, which surprised me. "Right on schedule. Didn't I tell you about Anton's Syndrome?"

"No."

"Harmless hallucinations. You know what a hallucination is?"

"Not really."

"It's a sensory experience of something that does not exist outside the mind."

"I was seeing something that wasn't there?" I could feel my world crumbling, my hopes gone.

"Don't look so confounded miserable! This means you're healing. Happens to people who've had their occipital lobes disturbed. That nerve is used to seeing things. If you've got a blanked-out area the brain will substitute. You'll be seeing a lot of things. Enjoy the scenery. You might see family, friends. Your house down on that island. And when people tell you they can't see what you see, just say, 'Too bad.'"

Over the next three or four days, I "saw" many images of the past. The Schottegat, with sailboats on it; Mount Sint Christoffelberg, the highest in Curaçao; the swinging pontoon bridge at the harbor entrance; my father; Stew Cat; even Henrik van Boven.

The hallucinations never came at the same time of day and I could not program them, couldn't order my mind to see something, then have it appear.

I think it was on the afternoon of the fourteenth day after the operation that I saw Timothy. He was standing in the water up to his knees, and I was certain he was at the south beach of our cay, though I'd never seen it, of course. He wasn't saying anything, just smiling at me.

I knew on that day that my curtain of darkness would soon roll back.

It happened in the early morning two days later. I awakened to an orange light in the room. The nurses had never drawn the blinds; there had been no need for that. The orange light filled the room and the walls were indeed green. I looked around, my heart thudding. *I can see*, I said to myself. *I can see . . .*

Just to test myself, I looked at the glass of water on the bedside table, then touched it. It was no Anton's Syndrome glass, no hallucination glass. It was real, full of water.

I jumped out of bed and went to the window and looked out. It was dawn over New York City. I saw skyline and streets and buildings and people and cars and trucks.

I whirled around and ran down the hall, shouting, *"I can see! Timothy, I can see! I can see."*

One of the night nurses grabbed me and said, "Yes, yes, yes . . . please hush . . ." and got me back to my room, where I sat by the window, just looking out, as the orange light of sunrise turned to yellow. I was seeing daylight for the first time since April.

The nurses called my mother and Dr. Pohl, and about a half hour later he rushed into the room, wearing a sweat shirt, his hair mussed. There were tears in the eyes of that rough, gruff man. I saw them, glistening like morning dew. He hugged me, murmuring, "Thank God, oh, thank God . . ."

24

The *Hato*

MARCH 1942—Timothy was trying to hold his temper in the King's Wharf office of Archibald and Sehade, Shipping Agents, St. Thomas, V.I. Archibald, a fat bald-headed *bukra*, sweating behind a big mahogany desk in his shirtsleeves, said, "Papa, why dontcha go back home an' sit in your rockin' chair on the front porch. You're too old to go to sea . . ."

"Ah only sold mah schooner two year ago," Timothy replied. "Ah sailed 'er till the day Ah sold 'er . . ."

"What's that got to do with today?"

"Yuh put up a poster on de wharf oskin' experienced men to go to sea 'cause o' de wahr . . ."

It was a War Shipping Administration poster, printed by the government: Merchant Seamen, The Allies Need You. Small print instructed local applicants to contact Archibald and Sehade, agents for the WSA.

"Ah bin to sea more'n fifty year," Timothy said, stubbornly.

"You look it," said Archibald, shuffling papers on his desk. Timothy's crinkly hair had turned white.

"Ah'm not oskin' to be a coptin . . ."

Archibald laughed. "I'm glad of that."

"Ah'll sign on as an AB." An able-bodied seaman.

In the oilskin packet in Timothy's hand were Coast Guard papers certifying him as both an able-bodied seaman and a master of sailing vessels up to five hundred tons.

Archibald sighed. "Papa, fightin' a war is a young man's game. You'd get in the way."

"Sirrah, don' call me Papa. My name is Timothy. Ah want to do mah part."

Archibald sighed again. "All right, Timothy. I might send you to a ship but I guarantee you the master'll refuse to sign you on. He'll tell you to go home an' sit in your rocker."

Timothy didn't reply, just stayed firmly in his chair across from Archibald, straw hat on his knee, papers resting on the other one.

"Show me watcha got," said Archibald.

Timothy carefully extracted both his master's license and the AB papers and passed them over to the agent.

Archibald frowned. "What's this 'unknown' for your date of birth? You don't know when you were born?"

"No, sir."

Archibald shook his head. "What do you think?"

"Oh, Ah'm sixty."

Archibald was writing on a slip of paper. "I should add ten to that."

Timothy remained silent. He remembered Wobert

Avril telling him to say he was sixteen when he shipped out on the *Gertrude Theismann* a half century ago. Now he'd claimed he was younger than he really was.

"Timothy Gumbs, that your right name?"

"Yes, sirrah."

Just before he got his own schooner, Charlie Bottle had taught him how to spell "Timothy Gumbs." Up to that time, he'd signed everything official with an *X*. But in his own mind, he was still just "Timothy," no last name.

"Okay, I'm sending you to a trampship called the *Hato*. She's tied up at the West Indian docks . . ."

Timothy knew the *Hato*. He'd seen her many times. She "tramped" around between Miami, Havana, Porto Rico, St. Thomas, Curaçao, and Panama, carrying whatever cargoes she could pick up. She was old and small, and that was fine. She looked clean, the sign of a good master.

"The captain told us yesterday he was short an AB."

Timothy nodded.

Archibald continued. "If he won't take you, don't bother me again. Go back to your front porch. If he does take you, you don't need to worry about getting hit with a torpedo. No German U-boat would waste one on a ship that small." He returned the papers.

"Ah thank yuh," Timothy said, rising. He went out into sunlight filtered by a rain shower.

He hadn't really been happy the last two years, since selling the *Hannah Gumbs*. He now thought he'd made a mistake by retiring. He missed going to sea. Playing dominoes with other old sailors up by the Market Place, listening to all the chatter, walking the waterfront, wasn't much of a substitute for weighing anchor and raising the sails, putting Flamingo Point to the stern. He wasn't ready for the rocking chair and didn't have a front porch. He lived in a boardinghouse on Torve Strade. At times he was quite lonely. At sea he'd never been lonely.

From the waterfront he could see the neat *Hato*, with a black hull and a white midships structure, tied up to the West Indies docks across St. Thomas harbor. He began the long walk on the curved road that flanked the harbor, hoping that the master of the *Hato* would be an elderly gentleman and appreciate the skills of a seasoned mariner.

An hour later, he stood opposite the little ship, studying her. She was working cargo, loading it, and even in that messy situation she remained tidy. He saw no rust on her, no streaks of oil, no frayed lines or tattered flags. For a trampship she'd had loving care. He nodded in satisfaction.

The *Hato*, registered out of Curaçao, owned by her Dutch captain, was 205 feet in length, 32 feet in width; 498 gross tons. Steel hulled, diesel powered. She'd been built in Hellevoltsluis, Holland, in 1921.

But Timothy had to agree with Archibald. Only a very hungry U-boat commander would attack her. She was like a minnow compared to the huge tankers that sailed in and out of Curaçao.

Timothy wished himself good luck and walked up her gangway.

Next morning, he helped heave in the stern lines as the *Hato* got underway for Curaçao, where she would load more cargo, then sail on to Panama.

25

The *Audaz Adventurero*

EARLY APRIL 1943—My father chartered the *Audaz Adventurero*, a sleek twenty-four-foot sloop, in Cristobal, and we stocked it with enough food and water for ten days, then set sail northwest across Clark Basin, the calm seas off Panama and Costa Rica.

A light breeze shoved us along at about four knots, the sloop behaving nicely. She handled well, my father said, and if the winds were favorable we'd arrive in the area where I thought the Devil's Mouth was located in about four days.

Excitement mounting hourly, I studied the chart laid out on the deck of the small cockpit well. En route, we'd pass the inhabited San Andres Island, the uninhabited Albuquerque and Bolivar cays, and other tiny islands, some dotted with palm trees. The sailing direction book describing them was by my knees.

My father was at the tiller, steering. The air was warm and the blue sea glistened. Far to the west, rolls of white clouds hung over Costa Rica's mountains.

Looking down at the chart, I said, "I wish we had time to visit all of them."

"So do I," he answered, eyes searching from beneath the bill of his baseball cap. He was worried about those uncharted coral reefs lurking just beneath the surface— the same worry that Captain Murry and Timothy had mentioned.

Earlier, I'd stood on the bow at lookout when we'd gone near some white-water reefs.

Cayo del Este sits on a coral bank about 24 miles northeast of Cayos de Albuquerque. The narrow island is about five hundred yards long and only four feet high. Cayo Bolivar is 1.25 miles west of del Este, and Cayo Arena 1.25 miles northwest of del Este. Fishermen's huts stood on these cays. Sailing directions said that a shipwreck was on Sudeste Reef, 3.25 miles northwest of Cayo Bolivar light. I wanted to see it. Maybe on another trip?

It would be fun, I thought, to spend a few days on each one. Exploring. Swimming. Fishing. Lying in the warm sand and looking up at the sky, daydreaming. Thinking about the shipwreck secrets of the tropic isles.

We were in Timothy territory. The farther northwest we sailed, the more I thought of him.

On this beautiful day, and actually for a long time now, I wished I could take back some of the things I'd said to him during the time on the raft and the first weeks on the cay. I'd called him ugly and stupid, laughed at him because he couldn't spell.

"He was probably the wisest man I'll ever know," I said, almost to myself.

"Who?" my father asked, glancing down at me, frowning.

"Timothy."

He nodded. "Wisdom comes in a lot of varieties."

Ashamed of myself, I hadn't told either of my parents how snotty and selfish I'd been with Timothy during the first days we were together. I'd told them about writing *HELP* in the sand with a stick because he couldn't spell it. Oh, I felt superior to him that day.

"A lot of people on this earth can't read or spell but that doesn't make them stupid," my father said. "You said he'd never gone to school."

"He hadn't."

"Can you imagine how embarrassed he was?"

I could now. An eleven-year-old kid telling him how to spell. He'd pretended to know, I remembered.

"I know people with college degrees who aren't wise. Being intelligent and being wise are two different things."

Thinking back, I believe I began to think of Timothy as wise the day he wove a rope of vines that would stretch from our hut down to the beach and fire pile. The vine rope was for me to make my way back and forth. I never would have thought of it.

Thinking back, I saw that scarcely a day went by that Timothy did not use his wisdom and experience so that I could survive.

I put the chart back inside the cabin, which had two bunks, a small galley with a kerosene stove, and storage spaces; then I went forward with the binoculars.

Having been blind, I no longer took sight for granted.

Before I became blind, eyesight was as natural as breathing. Now I realized just how precious it was. Even though my vision was 80 percent of normal, with glasses, everything seemed sharper, the colors brighter, than before. From the time I opened my eyes in the morning until I closed them at night, I appreciated everything I saw.

"Green turtle off the starboard bow," I yelled back to my father. I'd focused in on a big loggerhead.

The *Audaz Adventurero*'s wake boiled on northwest.

26

Torpedoed

APRIL 6, 1942—At about 2:20 A.M., in the darkest part of the night, with clouds covering the stars, the port lookout on the bridge of the long-range Nazi U-boat said, "*Ziel vorn*"—Target ahead—and read off the degrees. He'd seen diesel sparks in the blackness.

Instantly, four high-powered binoculars were focused on the dim outlines of a ship.

"She's not too big," said the watch officer, ordering speed decreased. Then he summoned the commanding officer from his bunk below.

In a few minutes the young *Kapitänleutnant* came up through the conning tower in his shorts and took a look, agreeing that the target was not as large as he would have liked. But his patrol had already been very successful.

He'd killed ten Allied ships, the last one a big tanker seven hours ago.

Low on fuel and food, he was headed home to the U-boat's base in Nazi-occupied Lorient, France, and had two greased torpedoes left in the bow tubes. Scanning the outlines of the ship, he decided to save one for the future and use one for this unexpected target. He sent the boat to battle condition. Ringing bells rudely awakened those who were asleep below. Half-naked men ran to their stations throughout the slim hull.

The First Officer always fired the torpedoes when the U-boat was surfaced, as it was now, and he was on the bridge within three minutes, yawning and rubbing his eyes.

The *Kapitänleutnant* said, "We take what we can get," almost apologizing for the size of the target. "Just use one. We can come in closer." The night would hide the submarine. Many of the Allied ships were still unarmed.

The U-boat began to maneuver to get into proper firing position.

At two o'clock Timothy had been relieved of bridge duties to go astern and spend the rest of the watch on the *Hato*'s fantail, on lookout. He'd steered for an hour, then stood bridge lookout for another hour.

He went by the galley to fix a cup of hot coffee and take it out on the stern. Because of wartime conditions and the U-boat menace, the captain had ordered nighttime lookouts fore and aft.

Timothy didn't mind the graveyard watch from

twelve to four because he didn't sleep all that much, anyway. Old age, again. He spent the time slowly pacing, watching the stars when the sky was clear, watching the flying fish spring out of the sea and glide away on the ship's passage.

The little ship was blacked out and everyone aboard was asleep, except those on watch. Timothy hadn't counted the passengers but thought there were seven or eight aboard. The *Hato* would discharge most of them in Panama. He'd heard several would go on to Miami, the ship's next port of call.

Timothy was glad to be back at sea, even if he wasn't on a sailing ship. The diesel engines in this one pounded, and the exhaust, swooping down from her stack, stank. But he felt the sea under his feet and by moving forward a few feet he could avoid the exhaust smell. It was good to be a sailor again.

Though it had been fourteen years since the *Hettie Redd* rolled over and came apart in the wild seas between Antigua and Nevis, seldom a week had gone by that he hadn't thought of Jennifer Rankin and the other passengers who'd drowned out there.

There'd been a British board of inquiry at Antigua, the members concluding that Captain Timothy Gumbs had not been advised that a hurricane was approaching. No warning had been issued by the port authorities. Therefore, he was not responsible for the sinking of the *Hettie Redd*. The hurricane was a weather condition over which Captain Gumbs had no control.

But Timothy clearly knew he shouldn't have sailed that day. The glassy look of the sea, the heat, the smell of the air, the gathering clouds, all told him he shouldn't sail. He'd gambled and lost.

On nights such as this one, he thought of beautiful Jennifer Rankin, grieved for those who had died, and asked to be forgiven.

———

The U-boat's First Officer shouted that the forward starboard torpedo tube was ready, bow cap off. It was wet, and the torpedo needed only the impulse from the bridge to be unleashed.

"Bridge control," said the First.

The attack sight, the target bearing transmitter, was on, the *Hato* in the center of the crosswires, aimed just aft of the midship house.

"Lined up," said the First.

The *Kapitänleutnant* nodded. Everything was going well. He knew that within a few seconds the attack table would be connected with the gyrocompass and the attack sight. After that, it was almost automatic. So long as the crosswires of the attack sight held the target, the apparatus would do its job.

The torpedo was set at a running depth of twelve feet, to tear out the target's bottom. Speed of thirty knots.

"Stand by for surface fire. Fire at five hundred meters . . ."

The order was acknowledged from below. "Tube One ready . . ."

The *Kapitänleutnant* said, "Fire when ready . . ."

The First Officer intoned, "Ready, on, on, on . . ." Finally, he said, "FIRE!"

The firing button was pushed, the torpedo motor started, and two seconds later the "eel" was on its way toward the *Hato*.

The *Kapitänleutnant* looked at his stopwatch and counted aloud. An orange ball lit the dark sea, followed by a *boom*.

"*Perfekt*," he said.

Timothy was thrown to the deck by the explosion that drove the *Hato* sideways, and even before he could stagger up, the oil drums on the afterdeck were exploding, lighting the night with fire. A wall of it raged between where he was and the bridge. He heard yells and screams, and the agony of shearing steel.

He hesitated a moment, trying to think how he could get around the wall of fire and help those people midships. He knew they'd try to launch a lifeboat. But the flames grew hotter and higher. Abandon ship was all he could do.

The starboard stern life raft, sitting on a wooden incline, poised to drop into the sea, had already been launched by the impact of the torpedo. In the red light that surrounded the ship he saw it about fifty feet off the stern, and he climbed up on the after rail, diving down.

Surfacing, he swam toward the raft.

27

The Cay

Our first stop, Isla de Providencia (13° 21′ north latitude, 81° 22′ longitude west), together with Isla Santa
Catalina, rose silently as we approached, shaped like a
sweet potato about ten miles long and three wide, taking
in several cays, one of which was palm covered. Low
mountains were on both islands.

Under a hot noon sun we soon anchored in Catalina
Harbor, where the water was so clear you could see crabs
crawling on the white-sand bottom. Bright-colored fish
swam by. Nearby were a half dozen sea-worn turtle
schooners. No one aboard them.

Looking around, my father said, "I don't believe this.
We have to be at the edge of the world." I felt the same.

We'd gone to a strange place that few people knew
of, a place so remote that its owner, Colombia, cared
little about its existence. Neither did any other nation.

It was just a tiny blue shape on a nautical chart. Two flashing lights marked it.

Several hundred yards away, on the beach, was streetless Isabel Village, a collection of weather-beaten shacks where the turtle fishers lived. There was little sign of life as we paddled ashore in our rubber dinghy. But life did exist there, thirty or forty grizzled fishermen.

The brown and black men of Isabel cackled and shook their heads when my father said we wanted to go to the Devil's Mouth. "Why go dere?" they asked.

"Dass right, why go dere?" they said. "Dom cays not wort de time 'n trubble . . ."

"Take some pictures," my father said.

The men cackled again. "Take pitchers cays 'roun' ere." Palm, Basalt, Low.

"Take Split Hill, Morgan Head, Alligator Point."

"Dass right."

It was not until my father said we'd pay for a guide that several became interested. Then coins were flipped.

———

Two days later, I stood on the bow of the *Audaz Adventurero* as it sailed northeast from Providencia. The weather hadn't changed, still sunny and warm. A few high white clouds were to the west over Nicaragua, just enough breeze to belly-out the mainsail and jib. The sea was indigo, five or six shades darker than the sky's blue. A beautiful day in the tropics. War was not talked of or thought about.

White-haired Egaltine Evermond, the turtle fisher we'd hired, stood with the tiller between his knees, silently looking out from beneath his battered straw hat. My father sat beside him. Captain Evermond was taking us to Boca de Diablo, the Devil's Mouth. He didn't know why he was taking us. He didn't care. Fifty dollars and a bottle of rum were what brought him there.

Caribbean sun had turned his wrinkled blackness into chocolate. He was a small man, missing most of his teeth; we'd guessed he was in his sixties. But his eyes were fish-hawk sharp. He said he'd been netting green turtles since he was big enough to climb into a "cotboat." He was from Grand Cayman Island, to the northeast.

By midmorning I knew we were getting near the horseshoe of coral that harbored Timothy's cay. I didn't know how I knew it. I just felt it, the way you feel the neighborhood in which you live.

About forty minutes later, Captain Evermond said, "Boca de Diablo," and nodded ahead. We were coming in from the east, the same way the raft had drifted.

Taking off my glasses, I put the binoculars to my eyes. Tops of palm trees clustered on the horizon. The island wasn't visible as yet.

My heart began to thud as I counted the palms. If there were fifteen, it was my cay, our cay. I knew there were fifteen because I'd climbed each one. I could only count seven now but I knew others were tucked in behind them.

My father was standing. "Is that it?"

"I think so." My heart drummed.

The *Audaz Adventurero* seemed to be creeping along, but slowly the island grew. First the palms, then the whiteness of sand below them, rising to what Timothy had said was the height of the island, about twenty feet.

I put the binoculars down and wiped my eyes. The lenses were fogging up. My hands shook.

I shouted back to them, "I'm sure that's it! . . ."

When I looked through the binoculars again I saw the hut to the right of the palms.

"It is!" I shouted. "I see the hut!" Though I'd only touched it before, I was certain it was the one I'd rebuilt.

My father joined me on the bow and took a look. "This cay's smaller than the one you described."

Timothy had told me it was about a mile long and a half mile wide. Now that I saw it, it was less than a half mile long and less than a quarter mile wide. I suddenly realized he'd done that on purpose, to make me feel better about being there. I wondered what other little lies he'd told me to push away fear.

Now, I could see some low brush and sea grape. "'Tis a beautiful cay, dis cay," Timothy had said. He was right.

Soon, we were within a hundred yards and the water was becoming shallow, coral heads visible beneath us. I only glanced at them, held by the sight ahead.

Captain Evermond shouted, "Drop de anchor!" and I tossed the Danforth over the side as the mainsail came down. My father quickly lowered the jib and within a few minutes the sloop rode at anchor.

"Go," my father said, and I passed the binoculars to him, grasped my glasses in my right hand, and dove.

Even the warm water tasted the same as I kicked toward the beach. Finally, my feet hit bottom. I remembered a little shelf and was glad I had tennis shoes on. Sea urchins lived on that shelf and their sharp spines were painful.

I waded in and took off my sneakers, digging my toes into the familiar warm, soft sand. I saw the remains of my fire pile. Nine months of wind had not entirely erased the charred wood.

I walked along east beach, remembering, remembering.

Then I went uphill, to the palm trees and our crude but strong hut, and Timothy's grave.

I looked down. The coral stones and shells were still where I'd left them.

I stood there for a little while, feeling very close to him, shut my eyes, then said, "Dis b'dat outrageous cay, eh, Timothy?"

On the wind that was rustling the palms I thought I heard laughter, and a voice from above that said, "Dis be it, Phill-eep . . ."

I wasn't dreaming.

Reader Chat Page

1. After he is rescued, Phillip decides to risk a serious operation so that he might see the cay where he was stranded for three months. Why do you think Phillip wants to return so badly? Do you think it's a good idea? Explain.

2. When Phillip first meets Timothy, he looks down on him because of the way he talks and because he can't read and write. But as he gets to know the older man, Phillip realizes that Timothy is an incredibly smart man. What do you think makes someone intelligent?

3. As a young man, Timothy lies about his age to become the cabin boy on the *Gertrude Theismann*, and as an old man, he pretends to be younger so that he can join the crew of the SS *Hato*. How do you feel about his lies? What are the consequences of his choices?

4. Phillip is only eleven, but his parents allow him to make the decision about whether to have life-threatening brain surgery to restore his vision. Do you think the risks of death, brain damage, and infection are worth the slim chance of Phillip regaining his sight? Do you think Phillip is old enough to make a life-and-death decision?

5. For the rest of his life, Timothy regrets going out to sea on the day the *Hettie Redd* sank. Is it his fault that the boat sinks? Is there any truth to his superstitions?

6. Phillip and Timothy couldn't be more different, yet they become dear friends. Have you ever become friends with someone who was very different from you?

7. In his first job as a sailor's apprentice, Timothy tries to prove himself by climbing the two-hundred-foot-tall mast of the *Gertrude Theismann*. But halfway up the mast, he becomes petrified with fear, too scared to climb another step on the ladder. Have you ever had a lofty goal only to stop in your tracks because of anxiety or fear? What can you do to overcome your fear and achieve that goal?

8. Both Timothy and Phillip have dreams that seem impossible at first. Phillip dreams of being able to see again, and young Timothy dreams of being a ship captain against all odds. What do you think motivates each of them to keep his dream alive, and in what way does each contribute to his own success?

9. As a boy of fourteen, Timothy leaves everything he knows behind so that he can pursue his dream to become a sailor, and blind Phillip survives alone on the cay for weeks until he is finally rescued. Are independence and self-reliance inherent qualities, or are they skills learned as a result of necessity as people get older?